SPECIAL MESSAGE TO READERS

This book is published under the auspices of

THE ULVERSCROFT FOUNDATION

(registered charity No. 264873 UK)

Established in 1972 to provide funds for research, diagnosis and treatment of eye diseases. Examples of contributions made are: —

A Children's Assessment Unit at Moorfield's Hospital, London.

•

Twin operating theatres at the Western Ophthalmic Hospital, London.

•

A Chair of Ophthalmology at the Royal Australian College of Ophthalmologists.

•

The Ulverscroft Children's Eye Unit at the Great Ormond Street Hospital For Sick Children, London.

You can help further the work of the Foundation by making a donation or leaving a legacy. Every contribution, no matter how small, is received with gratitude. Please write for details to:

THE ULVERSCROFT FOUNDATION,
The Green, Bradgate Road, Anstey,
Leicester LE7 7FU, England.
Telephone: (0116) 236 4325

In Australia write to:
THE ULVERSCROFT FOUNDATION,
c/o The Royal Australian and New Zealand
College of Ophthalmologists,
94-98, Chalmers Street, Surry Hills,
N.S.W. 2010, Australia

THE LACEY INHERITANCE

After her great-aunt's death, Penny learns that the old lady has left her a large sum of money in her will — provided that she successfully runs a market stall for a year! Penny isn't afraid of the challenge, but someone tries to make it difficult for her; first her stall is pulled down and then some of her paintings are deliberately damaged. Could the culprit be her cousin Max? Penny is determined to gain her inheritance if only to wipe the sickly smile off his handsome face . . .

DINA McCALL

◆

THE LACEY INHERITANCE

Complete and Unabridged

LINFORD
Leicester

First published in Great Britain in 1991

First Linford Edition
published 2003

British Library CIP Data

McCall, Dina
  The Lacey inheritance.—Large print ed.—
Linford romance library
  1. Love stories
  2. Large type books
  I. Title
  823.9'14 [F]

ISBN 0–7089–4928–2

Published by
F. A. Thorpe (Publishing)
Anstey, Leicestershire

Set by Words & Graphics Ltd.
Anstey, Leicestershire
Printed and bound in Great Britain by
T. J. International Ltd., Padstow, Cornwall

This book is printed on acid-free paper

1

'But it's quite ridiculous — what do I know about street markets?'

In that high-ceilinged room at Lacey Court, which had belonged to my lately-deceased Great-aunt Penelope, I stared with indignation at the other occupants. They looked back at me with expressionless faces; very much like those in the heavily-framed portraits on the walls. I had the feeling that they were all ranged against me, drawn together in mutual resentment. And the only person on my side was my darling Simon.

Trust the Laceys to give me no hint of what the bombshell had meant. Max Lacey even had the suspicion of a crooked smile on his lean and — I had to admit it — handsome features. Unmistakable Laceys, all of them, except for Mr Tunbridge, the family

1

solicitor, who looked like something out of Dickens.

The last time I'd seen them I'd been barely out of pigtails, but I recognised my distant relatives without any difficulty. The woman in the corner, hands folded on her lap and feet neatly tucked in, was, of course, my second cousin, Margaret. Fair and timid, she looked little older than she had been then, in spite of being a widow and a mother. Perched next to her on a narrow high-backed chair that looked too flimsy to take his weight, was her brother Brian Lacey. He was darker, but with the same grey eyes and high cheekbones. Heavily built and with an amiable face, he looked the most approachable of them all.

And then, dressed in a most unsuitable black leather jacket, his eyes a wary, darker grey, sat their elder brother — Max.

It was Max who spoke, now. Swivelling round in the big leather armchair where he had flung himself with accustomed ease — as well he might since Lacey Court now belonged to him — he countered my objection.

'Grandmother Penelope knew what she was doing. She always did,' he offered lazily.

'It's ridiculous!' I repeated weakly.

There seemed to be no other word for it. To be told I had inherited the greater portion of my great-aunt's estate was a shock enough — especially with her Lacey grandchildren staring at me and surely wishing I would drop dead on the spot. But to be told that I inherited only if I fulfilled a crazy stipulation — that was completely weird.

I drew in a deep breath and faced the solicitor. 'Can I think about it?'

Mr Tunbridge's narrow face flushed with annoyance, and he scooped some papers off a low coffee table and packed them back into his briefcase.

'I'm sorry — but it has to be today.'

'But what difference can it make?' I objected shrilly. 'You can't expect me to make such a decision right here and now . . . '

With a sigh he fished inside the briefcase, and took refuge in unfolding my great-aunt's will yet again, clearing his throat importantly.

'*I give devise and bequeath all the remainder of my estate wheresoever and whatever to my great-niece and namesake, Penelope Rossi . . . PROVIDED . . . provided that . . .* '

That was when Simon butted in. He was my fiancé, and as such he had been allowed to attend this family gathering, but until now had remained silent, listening to Mr Tunbridge intently and ignoring the sardonic glances of Max Lacey, and the frankly curious ones of Brian and Margaret.

'We know all that, old man,' he said. 'But let's cut the frilly stuff, shall we?'

I winced, seeing Max's eyebrows rise. Not everyone appreciated Simon's manner. He was as different from my Lacey relations as could possibly be, ruddy-haired and blue-eyed, with a

4

profile occasionally described by a kindly critic as being like a Greek god. And if he was a little, well, shall we say impetuous at times, it was only his artistic temperament coming out. Simon was an actor. Not only that, but an actor/manager. Not a very well-known one perhaps, not as yet. But well on the way. I warmed to him, thankful that he at least would look after my interests.

'Stop me if I've got it wrong,' he was saying. 'But does this mean that Penny cops the lot?'

'Er — ' Mr Tunbridge's lips thinned into a line, as he worked this one out. 'That is correct,' he conceded at last, looking down his nose at Simon with an expression of distaste. 'After payment of the legacies, of course, which have been fairly substantial . . . '

'Grandma's done us all proud,' Brian agreed genially. He smiled at me. 'No need to feel bad about it, Penny. She's helped us all in our time. Now it's your turn.'

'But Penny doesn't get anything,' Simon interrupted doggedly, 'unless she takes over some crumby market stall — '

'Takes it over, and runs it successfully for a year,' Margaret added in her breathless little voice. Then she flushed, and coughed, and subsided into silence.

'Oh yes — she has to get her pretty hands dirty,' Max chuckled, with a wicked sideways glance at me. 'That's how Grandmother began, before she netted one of the gentry as a husband. She always considered her humble beginnings to have been character building. We've all had to do our stint, in return for favours in the past.'

He paused, reflecting, his mouth curved with amusement. 'I think she was right, at that.' He looked at me directly then. 'She obviously considered that her great-niece needed a dose of the same.'

I ignored him and glanced hopefully at Simon, who was not looking at me but was chewing the edge of one of his fingernails thoughtfully. I didn't want to be reminded of what Great-aunt Penelope had said about me. Or to consider what Max Lacey thought about me. The whole thing was out of the question. Anybody could see that. Simon would agree with me, I felt sure. Max was laughing at me. He'd always laughed at me, I remembered resentfully.

'As I was saying,' I said stonily. 'The whole thing is quite ridiculous. I don't know anything about open-air markets, and I have no intention of being some kind of . . . of . . . '

'Barrow boy?' Max offered.

Simon leaned across and took my hand. 'Does anyone mind if my fiancée and I leave the room for a few minutes private conversation?'

They all shook their heads. I couldn't see what we had to talk about, but he gave my hand an impatient little tug, so I rose to my feet.

'We shan't be long,' I said with

dignity, and followed him out into the hallway.

'Darling . . . have you ever heard such rubbish?' I began, expecting him to take me in his arms in agreement, but he hardly listened.

'Let's go in here, shall we?' he said, opening another door and peering round it. 'Dining room, isn't it?'

'Yes,' I said. 'And good heavens . . . all laid out ready.'

'Max Lacey certainly knows how to do us proud, I'll say that for him, even if he is the kind of sarcastic git that gets right up my nose.'

For once his plain speaking irritated me. It seemed out of place in that lovely room with its long dining table already laid with a snowy-white cloth, and plates piled high with ham and tongue, tiny golden sausage rolls, great bowls of different kinds of salads, tomatoes red and shining, spring onions sticking up spikily from their glass containers.

'Why did we have to come out here?'

I complained. 'I was just about to tell them what to do with their precious Lacey money . . . '

'Are you mad?'

I stopped, shocked by the tone of his voice. He had never spoken to me like that before. He sounded impatient . . . and almost scornful. Simon saw that he had gone too far, and slid an arm around my shoulders, drawing me close. 'It's a lot of money, Penny my love,' he reasoned.

'Money isn't everything,' I murmured, still upset by his manner. 'I never expected anything, so I won't miss it now. You can't seriously think I'm going to stand all day in a market, selling things?'

'Sweetie . . . now look.' He nuzzled at my neck in the way he knew I liked, and his voice became persuasive. 'You know this play is gobbling up money. We only need to keep it going another few months, then who knows, a London season perhaps?'

He bent his head and kissed me

tenderly. As I responded with enthusiasm I found myself thinking disloyally — so he wants me to finance his production, does he? Then I thought, well — why not? Perhaps then, at last, he would agree that we could be married. It had been talked over between us often enough, but somehow something always seemed to get in the way. He wanted me to have security, he said. Great-aunt Penelope's money would provide that — for both of us. And perhaps a market stall might be quite a giggle, if we took it on together. The Laceys obviously thought I couldn't do it — and that was enough to make me want to give it a go.

'If you really want me to,' I began. 'If you could work your days to suit, then we could — '

He sprung away from me as if he'd been stung. 'But, Penny, darling,' he said amazed. 'You must be joking. I simply wouldn't be able to help. I haven't the time for a start, and anyway — '

Anyway, he wouldn't contemplate doing such a thing, even if he had all the time in the world! The fact that I had been equally horrified a moment ago conventially slipped my mind. My rose-tinted spectacles toppled from my nose in one sudden rush, and I was seeing Simon clearly for the first time — his affected mannerisms, his studied good-looks, his pseudo-bolshy frankness, and his obvious eye for the main chance.

I had confidently expected him to back me up, whatever decision I made, but it seemed I was on my own. I felt tears spring to my eyes, hot and angry.

'So you won't help me?' I demanded.

'It's not that I won't. It's just that I can't — '

'Get *your* pretty hands dirty, either.'

He flushed. 'There's no need to be like that.'

I forced a sweet smile, and watched the relief spread across his face.

'No — you're quite right,' I agreed.

'I'll just tell them, I don't want the legacy.'

His relief turned once more to alarm. 'But, Penny . . ?'

I felt my cheeks burning, and I knew that the Italian part of my blood was taking over, but I didn't care. I could not bear to look at Simon for one moment longer. I stamped my foot and screamed at him.

'Get out of here, Simon. Get out now!' I looked around wildly for something to throw.

'But, Penny . . ?' His desperation was becoming obvious.

'Don't 'but, Penny' me, you — you wimp, you! Get out and stay away from me. I don't ever want to see you again.'

The first thing that came to hand was a small ormolu clock on the mantel-piece, and I snatched it up, raising my arm. With a yelp of alarm Simon turned and fled. I heard the front door close after him, and then his car start up.

I don't think I really meant to throw the clock. I just stood there, trembling with temper, and disillusionment, feeling a complete fool. I could imagine what Max Lacey would say. Well, I'd show him. I'd show them all!

I left the dining room, closing the door quietly behind me, and took time in the wide hall to check my appearance.

I was quite different from the Laceys. Great-aunt Penelope and my grandmother had been twins, but after that the family lines had diverged. My mother had kicked over the traces and caused quite a furore in the family by running away with an Italian Count. So, whereas the Laceys carried on the firm sharp features of their forebears, I had inherited the thick, dark hair that stood out from my head in stubborn curls, from my father. From him, too, I inherited my olive skin and brown eyes — and my temper.

I smoothed my skirt over my hips, and tucked my high-necked white sweater in a little more neatly. Black skirt and a black and tan dog's-tooth checked jacket, those were my only concessions to the occasion of Great-aunt Penelope's funeral. After all, although I had been named after her, I hardly knew my aged relative. Certainly she had seen little of me, and not enough to say the nasty things that had been read out in the will —

At the memory I burned again. I felt in my pocket and brought out a slim compact. A touch of powder cooled my cheeks. I needed no lipstick, my lips were red enough, and rather too full for my liking. They gave me a sultry look that had often landed me in situations that were hard to control. Still, today I felt I appeared business-like and capable, and that was how I needed to be.

I opened the big doors to the sitting room, and they all looked up. They seemed to have been sitting without speaking, deep in thought. Had they heard my screaming match with Simon, I wondered?

I walked without undue haste to my

14

vacant chair, and sat down, giving each of them a composed smile.

Cousin Margaret looked towards the door. 'Where's your fiance?'

'He had to leave,' I said pleasantly. 'He asked me to give you his regrets.'

Mr Tunbridge showed no surprise. 'Have you come to a decision?' he asked a little wearily.

I nodded. 'I'll do it,' I said decisively. 'I'll take over the market stall. *And*,' I added with emphasis and a defiant look at Max, 'I'll make a profit with it.'

'Oh, Penny-wise!' Max Lacey murmured, and his grey eyes were mocking.

★ ★ ★

The sausage rolls were just as delicious as they looked. We'd all trooped into the dining room once Mr Tunbridge had taken his leave, pleading another engagement and obviously glad to see the back of us. I don't think he had enjoyed his task and was grateful to escape.

'It's not usual to read the will out in this way,' Max said casually, as though reading my thoughts. 'But Grandmother specifically instructed that it should be done. Have a pickled onion.'

I didn't answer him, but piled my plate up with goodies and sat down on the long, low window seat, beside Margaret.

'How are the children?' I asked. 'Two boys, isn't it?'

'Oh — they're fine.' Her face became quite animated. 'Peter is six now, and Charlie four — and proper little rascals.'

I nodded, and leaned back, preparing myself for a long session of mother-love. As I absent-mindedly tucked into my plateful of food I reflected how little time had changed Margaret. She always had been obsessively attached to someone — first her parents, then her brothers, then her husband Howard until his untimely heart attack. Now it was her children. That was natural enough, I suppose.

Her brother, Brian, was at the other end of the room, his broad back to me. He was talking to Max. Were they discussing me, I wondered? They must all have been rather taken aback to find how much had been left to me. Not that they had been in any way left out of the will. On the contrary Max had been left the house and grounds, and Brian shares in the pottery business that had been started by his grandfather. And Margaret — well Margaret had £15,000 — but did she think that enough?

Probably not. What was she wittering on about now? Something to do with the price of shoes. I nodded wisely.

'Children are expensive,' I murmured, hoping the remark would fit.

'Oh I do so agree,' she gasped. 'And of course Howard intended them to go to Abbeystoke School when they were older . . . but I don't know now . . . '

Her voice tailed off, and a quick glance showed her cheeks pink and her hands trembling.

'Did your grandmother know that?' I queried.

She shook her head. 'Not that it matters,' she said brightly. 'I believe the local comprehensive is a very good school.'

My appetite was disappearing, and making an excuse I left her and returned my plate to the table. It wasn't my fault that Great-aunt Penelope had left me the bulk of her estate. Of course, I could help Margaret — and I would. But that wasn't the point, was it?

I found Brian Lacey at my side. For a large man he moved very quietly. 'I suppose I should offer my congratulations,' he said with a grin that persuaded me he meant it. 'On your inheritance, I mean.'

I was glad it wasn't on my engagement, because that was definitely all over.

'Do you mind very much?' I asked frankly. 'I mean . . . I can't think why she chose me.'

'Can't you?' He looked at me a little oddly, and then as if deciding something, said, 'I expect she was feeling a little guilty.'

'Guilty?' I was taken aback. I hadn't expected that. 'But she hardly knew me. I only ever came here once.'

The only time I'd been to Lacey Court was seven years ago, when I was 16. Until then I'd lived in Italy, where my mother had found that being a Countess does not necessarily mean an easy life. I'd found that, too, though in my case it was not the lack of money that irked, but the lack of freedom. The intimacy of my Italian relations was claustrophobic, my movements, too, curtailed. Above all, I wanted to spread my wings.

And then my mother and father had a tiff, and she had decided to visit Lacey Court.

'Time you got to know your English family,' she had said, and straight away carted me across Europe with this in mind.

I had been delighted. I loved England, and in particular Lacey Court. I adored the green countryside, the dogs that played with me, the ponies I could ride. But my great-aunt had scared me.

I said as much to Brian, and he laughed. 'Her bark was worse than her bite.'

'Her bark was more than enough for me!'

I wondered whether he had been told about the incident that had sent Mum and me scurrying away — my mother back to Italy, and myself to London and a job — our tails between our legs. Perhaps not. But then he must have wondered what she had meant by the will . . .

I regret that my sister's grandchild has been neglected. Her behaviour has proved to me that the mixture of blood on that side of the family was ill advised. She needs discipline. And where better to find that, than working in the market?

Penelope Lacey, had been small, round and indomitable. When I knew her she reminded me of Queen Victoria. It was hard to imagine her as pretty and vivacious enough to capture anyone's heart. They said my Great-uncle found her winsome, and had returned to the market every day for three months before he had won her. There was nothing winsome about her on the last occasion I had seen her.

Even before that dreadful day, I had regarded her with caution — she was too high-powered for me. However, my second cousins had been another matter. Margaret, at that time, I admired. She had long pale hair, and with her height and slender looks could wear clothes beautifully. Not like me. I was already rounding out and developing the kind of figure that made the boys turn their heads. I would much rather have been like Margaret.

Brian, I had liked. He was easy to talk to, always the mediator, too lazy to be awkward. He had taken the time to ride with me. Not too proud to be seen with a child of 16.

'Are you sure you don't want a pickled onion?'

I was wrenched back to the present day with a jerk, and swung around, ready to wither Max Lacey with a glance. But something stopped me. He was so assured, casual in that leather jacket so unsuitable for a funeral — not looking at all the successful business-man I believed him to be. His grey eyes were alight with amusement. *He* remembered times past, there was no doubt about that!

What he forgot was that I was no longer a 16-year-old girl.

'Ah, Max,' I said lightly. 'The perfect host, as ever.'

'I do everything I can to please,' he murmured. 'Almost everything, at least.'

I could feel the anger seething through me, but I was damned if I would give him the satisfaction of showing that I knew what he was talking about.

I picked up my plate again, and gave a very creditable performance of enjoying a sandwich. 'Tell me,' I said between bites. 'What am I supposed to be selling on this stall of Great-aunt's — and where is the stall, anyway?'

'The actual equipment is in one of the outhouses here.' A small smile quivered, as though he was relishing the fact that I was deliberately blocking him. 'As for what you sell — well that is up to you.'

'Oh . . . ' I was startled. I had somehow thought everything would be laid on, and all I had to do was walk into a market and start taking money. I could see it would be a little more complicated. 'What did Margaret sell, when she did it?'

'Garden gnomes.'

'What!' I nearly dropped my plate in surprise, and he laughed.

'I assure you. She made them, too. Horrid little things.'

I looked across at Margaret with some respect. I had imagined her selling baby clothes, or baskets of dried flowers. Not making and lugging about great lumps of concrete. 'And you?'

'Brian dealt in garden supplies. I had a go with tools, spare parts for cars, anything like that.'

Yes . . . I remembered now. He had built it up into a business eventually. A very successful one, hiring out equipment to the DIY car mechanics. So I was on my own. The idea was daunting.

I tilted up my chin and stared defiantly into those cool eyes. 'And when do I have to start?'

'There's no hurry.' He folded his arms, surveying me with an interest I found insolent. 'The year will run from when you start trading. We wouldn't want to throw you in at the deep end without a few tips on how to go about it.'

I was sensible enough to show gratitude. 'Thank you.' The words stuck in my throat. In my opinion I had little enough to thank Max Lacey for.

'Of course you will stay here,' he announced.

I was astounded at the cheek of him. 'That won't be necessary. I'll find somewhere.'

'Nonsense. Why waste money? Stay here. There's plenty of room.' He looked straight into me, to the confusion, the embarrassment, the anger.

'Don't worry,' he said gently. 'I'll stay out of your way — if that's what you want.'

Then, having finished with me, he tapped his brother on the shoulder, and he and Brian moved away to continue their conversation. I was left seething.

Max Lacey — the cause of my shame, my banishment. The man I detested — and the man I had fallen so headlong in love with, when I was only 16.

2

Three months after the reading of the will, I was drawing up to Lacey Court in a battered old van, wondering what kind of reception I was going to get.

There had been so much to do. Breaking off my engagement to Simon, for a start. That had not been easy, but I knew it was something I must do. For months I had been deluding myself, but now I realised that there could never be anything between us. It had taken a while for me to get through to Simon that I really didn't want to see him any more. He turned nasty, and I knew it was the inheritance he was regretting, more than me. It was a relief when it was finally over.

Next, I had to hand in my notice at the art gallery where I had worked ever since I'd decided to stay in this country. Only 16, and I'd found the job myself and had been justifiably proud of it. Mother had been doubtful at first, but I had persuaded her that I would be quite safe on my own, and at last, after seeing me safely sharing a flat with a couple of other girls, she had left me. I'd worked behind the scenes at first, helping to clean up the workshops, learning how to make frames, and finally had moved on to restoration and even the occasional touching up of paintings. I had enjoyed it, and I was sorry to go. But there it was — if I wanted my inheritance I had no choice.

I must say they were very good about it, and said there would always be a place for me, if things didn't work out.

I might well need it, I thought glumly, as I turned in through the big iron gates. This market-stall caper was not going to be as easy as I had first imagined.

For a start, it had taken me weeks to decide what I was going to sell. Finally in desperation, after once more turning the problem over without any result, I made a long-distance phone call to my mother.

'But cara mia, darling' she'd enthused with her usual careless mixture of language. 'What a wonderful opportunity for you. To inherit a fortune!'

I'd smiled fondly, knowing that her mind was already ticking over, weighing up the possibilities. I made myself comfortable on the settee, cradling the phone under my chin as I plumped up the cushions. Phone calls to my mother could take some time. Lucky I'd made it a transfer charge!

'I won't inherit anything unless I come up with some ideas pretty quickly,' I'd pointed out. 'And I'm sure Max Lacey would love that.'

'Oh . . . ?' I could hear the interest in her voice. 'What makes you think that?'

I shrugged. 'Just a feeling.'

She read my mind. 'You're not harking back to that silly incident, are you? All a misunderstanding, and you were only a child at the time. He'll have

28

forgotten all about it.'

I desperately wanted to change the subject. 'But, Mother — this dratted market stall. What am I going to sell?'

'Why . . . ' Her voice rose in amazement at my stupidity. 'You'll sell paintings, of course. What else?'

Trust my mother to hit on the obvious. Of course it must be oil paintings. What else did I know anything about? But I realised that on a market stall it would be no use offering old masters . . . or even the works of local artists, they would be too expensive.

Luckily I knew of studios that specialised in original oil paintings that were extremely cheap. That was what I had in mind, ideal for the market. But not rubbish . . . no, I would never offer that. I would only sell pictures that I could live with myself. These would be good . . . the kind of thing that ordinary people would enjoy having in their homes. With that aim in mind I had sat down to write to Mr Tui of Hong Kong.

Now at last, here I was. I had left it pretty late in the day. There'd been a lot of last-minute arrangements, and the sun was already setting when I drove up to the house. I took the van around the back and parked it. No need to unpack everything until morning. I just hoisted out my overnight bag and left the rest securely locked. Then I walked around to the side door of the house, knowing it was usually unfastened.

On the way I stopped for a moment, drinking in the scene. The sun was setting, and the creamy stone walls of the house glowed in the warmth of its reflected glory. The air was still, and fragrant. There was honeysuckle growing up the side of the porch. Farther along, at the front of the house, the walls were softened by creeper that would turn crimson in the autumn.

From the wood that curved away to the right of Lacey Court, an owl hooted.

Suddenly it caught me by the throat, that feeling of timeless beauty that made me almost want to cry. I had felt it before, when I was only a child. It had been a feeling of coming home, of belonging, such as I had never felt anywhere else. I hadn't been able to understand, or to handle it then . . . and it, as much as anything, had contributed to what had happened.

Now that I was grown up I was less likely to be swayed by such emotion. Or was I? What had made me accept Max Lacey's offer of accommodation, when I knew that living near him would be such an uncomfortable experience?

For a moment I nearly turned and walked back to the van, late though it was. I could have driven on to Malvern. No doubt I could have found a room somewhere . . . but then the door opened and Max was outlined in a bright shaft of light.

'Penny! I thought I heard your van arrive. Come along in. Did you have a good trip?'

I muttered something incoherent, as he came out and took the bag from my hand and I was hurried into the comforting warmth of the kitchen.

'Mrs MacDonald has gone home long since,' Max said. 'Sit down, I'll rustle you up something to eat.'

'There's no need . . . really.'

But I might as well have saved my breath.

Gradually, I relaxed, sitting back in one of the polished pine kitchen chairs, while he wasted no time but with deft economic movements slid a heavy frying pan on to the hotplate of the Aga. Soon the room was filled with the tantalising smell of sizzling bacon.

It shook me a little. Here was Max, waiting on me with every sign of good humour . . . and I had been expecting. what? My memory had turned him into an ogre. I had taken his invitation ungraciously, suspiciously — on my guard. Perhaps I had been completely wrong, and Mother had been right. The past was well behind me.

He had his back to me, and so I was able to study him at my leisure. He was

even more attractive than he had been
seven years ago. A little heavier perhaps.
The shoulders under his blue shirt were
somewhat broader, but the hips encased
in comfortably faded jeans were not. As
he bent over the stove his body was as
lithe, his movements as assured, as ever.
It annoyed me to feel a quickening of
my pulse, as though I was still that
impressionable schoolgirl . . . '

'How is Mrs MacDonald?' I asked.

He looked back over his shoulder, an
easy grin, his eyes warm with humour.
With the back of his hand he pushed
aside the thick, dark hair that had
flopped over his forehead.

'You know her . . . ruling us all with a
hand of iron.'

'And a heart of gold,' I added.

It had been Mrs MacDonald who
had held me when, sobbing and
distraught, I had fled from Great-aunt
Penelope's scathing tongue.

What a long time ago that had been,
and yet, sitting there it was as if the
intervening years had melted away. The

same red flagstones on the floor, a square of coconut matting at one side. The table was just as scrubbed. Slipping back into the old ways I rose from my seat and crossed to the pine dresser. There, in the drawer, I found the same cutlery. Things in Lacey Court didn't change much. But I had changed. I laid two places at the table.

'You *are* having something too, I hope,' I told Max. 'I hate someone staring while I eat alone.'

He chuckled as he loaded up the plates that had been warming. 'Unless you can manage eight slices of bacon and two eggs, I am.'

I pulled my plate towards me. 'Don't tempt me . . . this looks so good, I almost might.'

I tucked in, while he poured coffee into two of the brown mugs that had always hung on the dresser. The rich aroma blended with the smoky tang of the bacon. I gave a sigh of pleasure.

For a while we did not speak, but sat in companionable silence enjoying our supper. Then I spoke first.

'Where are Brian and Margaret?'

He looked surprised. 'At home, I imagine.'

Of course. What a fool I was, imagining the family still living here intact, as they had all those years ago. Time had not stood still. Margaret had married and left Lacey Court, and Brian . . . well, obviously Brian had moved out, too. But I wasn't going to let Max see what a silly mistake I had made.

'Of course home. But where might home be?'

His puzzled expression cleared. 'Oh . . . I forget you haven't really followed the fortunes of the family.'

'I never heard a thing about any of you,' I murmured. 'Not from the time I left. Not until the letter asking me to come here for the reading of the will.'

'And we never heard anything about you. What *did* you do after you left here?'

'Well, I didn't race straight to the

devil, in spite of what your grand-mother thought,' I replied tartly.

He didn't rise to the bait. 'Did you go back to Italy?' He sounded interested.

'Mother did . . . eventually,' I admitted. 'I found myself a job, and once she realised I was determined to stay, and was satisfied that I was all right, she left me here.'

He nodded, smiling. 'Yes . . . I remember you were very determined.'

'I still am.' What was it about him? Under that pleasant exterior there was a kind of awareness that he had not forgotten the past. But things were different now. I was not the child I had been then, and he was recognising it. I should have felt flattered, but rather it made me nervous.

'So . . . you were going to tell me about Brian and Margaret,' I persisted.

He leaned back in his chair, stretching out his long legs, folding his arms. 'Margaret and the children live in a small house on the edge of Lacey Court. Brian has a flat . . . a very smart one, in Malvern.' He stopped for a moment, and his eyes seemed to be looking through me, considering factors about which I knew nothing. 'On the whole,' he said slowly, 'it is perhaps just as well that they don't live here any more.'

I jumped to my feet, and collected up our used dishes, taking them to the sink.

'Why?' I challenged over my shoulder. 'Because of me? But they didn't seem to mind. About the inheritance, I mean. After all, Margaret seems quite settled, and Brian is doing very nicely with the pottery.'

'You really don't know anything . . . do you?'

It was so vehement, I was startled. I rinsed a plate under the tap carefully, and placed it in the rack. Then, tea towel in hand, I turned to face him. Was this the showdown I had expected, ever since I arrived?

'What is there to know? Great-aunt Penelope left me her money. I'm entitled to it. That's all I know, and as far as I am concerned, it's all that matters.'

It didn't come out at all as I had intended. It sounded hard and mercenary . . . and I hadn't wanted that. But Max had put me on the defensive again — and I learned very young that when cornered it is best to attack. This time, though, I'd bitten off more than I could chew. He jumped to his feet, and crossed the kitchen in two long strides to catch me by my shoulders. His grey eyes were dark and blazing, his face set. 'Isn't that just like you? You don't care about anyone but yourself . . . do you? You do what you want, and devil take the consequences.'

He could get mad, but I could get madder.

'And what do you know about me? You just jump to conclusions, don't you? You don't wait to find out what my intentions are. You aren't giving me a chance now.' Then I had to say those fateful words. 'Just like you never gave me a chance before.'

He let go of me, and took a step back to lean against the big deal table. He was smiling, but it wasn't a pleasant smile. It was far too knowing and cynical.

'I never gave you the chance you wanted, that's true enough.' He smirked.

'Oh . . . you!' My anger came blazing out now. 'You still persist in blaming me . . . even after all those years. Surely you can see now that I was speaking the truth. You didn't care . . . you didn't give me time to explain . . . '

One eyebrow raised. 'It didn't need much explanation, my dear. I may have been rather an unworldly young man in those days, but even I know what it means when I find a very nubile young girl in my bed!'

'You . . . you pig!'

I hurled the tea towel at his head, and then I dashed from the room. I ran up the broad curving staircase and along the carpeted gallery. Unthinking, I fled to the room at the far end. The one opposite Max's bedroom. The room that had been mine, seven years ago.

I didn't stop to ask myself whether this was the room that had been allocated to me. I just flung myself on the bed, and erupted into a bout of sobbing, part humiliation and part temper. Then I pulled myself together, sniffed, and found a hankie to dry my eyes.

Looking around me, I found that I had been right in my instinctive choice. This room had certainly been laid out ready for me. The bed was made up with a plump duvet in a pretty floral cover. There were clean towels hanging on a rail beside the wash basin, and on a little table beside the window stood a small vase of wild flowers.

Who had put them there? Mrs MacDonald? I doubted that. Kind though the housekeeper was, she was not the imaginative sort, and such a gesture would not have occurred to her. Neither would Margaret have thought of it, being too engrossed in her own family. No . . . it had to be Max. Besides which, he was the only one who knew how much I loved the flowers of the English hedgerows. It was just the sensitive, thoughtful touch that would come from him . . . as had been the meal he had prepared for me. He was still the Max I had known and loved . . . until he remembered how things had turned out. Then — like Great-aunt Penelope — he judged me, and still found me wanting.

Remembering my early days on that first visit to Lacey Court I recalled how Max and I had walked through the grounds then climbed over the fence into the fields beyond. Talking . . . always talking. He had known so much about the countryside, and I had known so little. I loved those morning rambles.

Cousin Margaret had talked about her family, and lent me clothes. Brian had been kind, and had ridden with me. But it was Max I idolised.

I blew my nose hard, and took myself

to task. The trouble was, I decided, coming here had made me feel as if I were that young girl all over again. It made me vulnerable, and unsure of myself, and I wasn't like that any more. I really should not let memories upset me. What on earth did it matter what Max Lacey thought about me? He was nothing to me, nor I to him. I was making a complete idiot of myself, all over again.

And, I discovered, I had left my bag downstairs. I couldn't even clean my teeth and go to bed until I fetched it.

Quietly I opened the door to my room, and listened. No sound. The landing lights were out. Max must have gone to bed. I felt my way down the stairs, and opened the kitchen door, feeling for the switch. The light flicked on, and I spotted my bag where I had left it.

Max could at least have brought it upstairs for me, I thought grumpily. But perhaps he'd been afraid to come near me with it. Thought I would be waiting to pounce on him, I thought cynically. Man-eater that's me . . . Huh! Perhaps he thought I wouldn't be satisfied with what his grandmother had left me. Perhaps he imagined I wanted him and Lacey Court as well!

It was the injustice of it that got me. When I had last visited Lacey Court I had been more of a child than they realised. I might have been fast developing those sultry looks that continued to give the wrong impression, but inside I was just a kid, looking for a hero.

In Max I thought I had found Him. I worshipped him, but it was all part and parcel of Lacey Court. I loved the whole place. And when my mother developed a sudden conscience about returning to Father, I couldn't face the thought of leaving.

She had sprung it on me suddenly, in the impetuous way she had of doing things, and I had been bereft. I couldn't go back to Italy . . . to that claustrophic atmosphere of a tight-knit, watchful, voluble family. And I couldn't leave Max. I adored him. I never made the mistake of thinking he would look on me as anything other than a young cousin to be kind to . . . but that was enough.

Somehow — I felt sure — somehow Max would help. I was confident that he would know what to do. He would find a way of persuading Mother to let me stay.

But he had been away from Lacey Court that day, and I had wandered around lost in misery while Mother did our packing. When it was time for bed, he still had not come home. I had to talk to him. It was so important.

So, I went to his bedroom to wait. And there, tired out with unhappiness and long hours of waiting, I fell asleep on his bed.

The next thing I knew was Great-aunt Penelope's horrified face looking down at me, and Max looking grimly at me over her shoulder — and all hell let loose.

The worst of it was, that it was Max who fetched her. Coming into his bedroom and finding me lying there, my skirt — so I was informed — rucked up; my hair — so I was told — wantonly spread across his pillow, he jumped to the wrong conclusion. Not even taking the risk of waking me up, he backed hastily out of the door and woke up his grandmother, who — like Queen Victoria — had not been amused.

I never really got the chance to explain. Mum and I were told we had outstayed our welcome, and only the fact that Mother was able to say truthfully that we were planning to leave anyway, saved our tattered remnants of pride. Smarting with embarrassment and mortification, I had turned my back on Lacey Court.

Now it seemed Max still held that same low opinion of me.

I sighed. Well — here I was, stuck by his invitation in his house, and there was nothing I could do about it. I was here for one purpose only, to prove I was worthy of my inheritance. And prove it I would! I'd show the lot of them.

Although it was late, I knew I would not be able to sleep for hours. My library book, I remembered, was in the van.

I fished the keys from the bag pocket, and unbolted the kitchen door. It was bright moonlight outside, and easy for me to see my way to where I had parked. I crossed the cobbled courtyard, sniffing appreciatively at the scent of the honeysuckle that still lingered on the cool night air. My spirits rose. Lacey Court was still beautiful, and provided I kept out of Max's way — which should not be difficult in a place this size — I would enjoy being back again.

I reached the van, and was about to unlock the driver's door, when I stopped, puzzled — and then horrified. The back doors of the van were thrown wide open, and on the cobbled stones of the courtyard, all around it, tossed about in the dark like so many pieces of unwanted rubbish, were the paintings I intended to sell. Somebody, filled with spite, had deliberately set out to damage my stock — to stop me from claiming my inheritance!

3

'It must have been you. Who else could it have been?'

Max and I faced up to one another in the courtyard, angry as two fighting-cocks. I'd woken early, not having had much sleep, after spending what seemed to me to have been half the night packing my spilt goods back into the van. I'd just stuffed everything in any old how, not having the heart to find out if there had been any damage. Then I'd spent more hours tossing and turning, and wondering why? For all that he disapproved of me, I'd never thought Max to be vindictive. And yet, what other explanation could there be?

Max glowered at me. He wasn't even properly clothed. I'd been up for ages, dressed ready for work in my jeans and a matching blue shirt, my hair tied back. I'd impatiently paced the corridor outside his room, and pounced the minute he put his nose outside his bedroom door. Protesting, he had tightened the belt around his dressing gown and gone back into his room for his slippers.

'I told you, I don't know what you're talking about.'

His hair was all tousled, his chin in need of a shave, and he looked not at all pleased, but completely bewildered, and far too attractive. Vulnerable, too, strangely enough.

I hardened my heart. 'I'm talking about my paintings. The stock I intend selling in the market.' I pointed at the van. 'The goods that were safely in the van when I arrived.'

He rubbed a hand through his hair. 'Paintings? You mean that's what you're going to sell? Rather high-flown for an open market, isn't it?'

'Don't be silly,' I said scornfully. 'I know what I'm doing. These come from the Far East . . .'

'Oh.' He curled his lip. 'I see. Funny,

I'd have thought you'd have better taste.'

He expected me to erupt, I could see that. But I wasn't going to give him the satisfaction. Besides which, he was simply trying to sidetrack me. We were getting away from the point, and I lost no time in bringing him back to it.

'I'm not interested in your opinion,' I said coldly. 'I just wanted to say that it was a pretty low-down thing to do. I don't know how you can stand there.'

'*What* was?' He shook his head and tutted at me. 'Really, Penny, my girl. You aren't very clear. It must be your foreign blood.'

I considered kicking him in the shins, but instead I took a deep breath.

'OK, Max, if you want it spelled out. In my van I had a lot of paintings, already framed and ready to sell. Last night I went outside to fetch my library book. I found half the paintings thrown all over the ground.'

I looked him straight in the eye. 'So what d'you say about that?'

He frowned, suddenly serious. Without speaking he walked up to the van and tried the back doors. 'Locked?'

'Naturally.'

He turned to me. 'But were they locked when you arrived? Can you be absolutely certain of that?'

I struggled to think back. 'Well, no, possibly not. They couldn't have been. Otherwise nobody could have opened them.'

'And were the doors properly shut?'

I could see the way his mind was working. I joined him, and unlocked the van, then showed him how the catch worked. 'Of course they were shut. I couldn't have driven here with them open now, could I?'

'No, but if you'd opened them here, and then not fastened them properly again. Well, suppose a dog, or a cat, was roaming about.' He demonstrated by leaving the door slightly ajar. 'It could have jumped in and knocked them out. A fox even.'

'Yes, but . . . '

I strained to think back. I was pretty sure I had not opened the back. My bag had been just behind me, and I'd lifted it across the front seats, hadn't I?'

'I think you'll find that's what must have happened,' he said lifting an eyebrow at me in a manner that was both quizzical and half amused. Then, having solved the mystery to his own satisfaction, 'Well, if that's all, I'll be getting back in. It's a bit chilly out here.'

He didn't give me the chance to press the matter any further, and I was left alone to prowl around the van, my thoughts even more disturbed and troubled than ever. I wanted his explanation to be the right one. And why . . . ? Because I was finding that Max Lacey still held a powerful fascination for me. There could be no other reason for my pulse racing in such a ridiculous fashion.

Things had not really changed, I admitted ruefully to myself, except that Max was even more attractive now than he had been when I was only a child. And if I had made a mistake in trusting him then, I would be making an even bigger one if I let him get under my skin again now.

I stood cursing my foolishness, and it was just as well for my peace of mind perhaps, that the housekeeper, Mrs MacDonald, arrived on the rickety old bicycle she always rode from her cottage at the end of the drive. She was as stocky as ever, sensible and down to earth in thick tweeds, her wiry grey hair standing on end with exertion, her eyes edged with laughter lines.

I stood quietly smiling, waiting for her to dismount, and she took me in her arms and gave me a bear hug. Then she pushed me away from her, and, holding my shoulders, gave me a little shake.

'Penny, my dear, so you made it — good. Sorry I was away before you arrived, but Tom was expecting his supper, you know how it is.'

Yes, I knew that her husband doted

on her, but refused to lift a finger to help himself, and had been like that for years, ever since he had been made redundant from the pottery. Mrs MacDonald didn't seem to mind, she just accepted him as he was.

'Anyway, Max looked after you, I hope?' she continued.

'Oh, yes,' I answered vaguely. 'Just fine.'

She gave me a quick, shrewd glance. 'So what are you doing out here at this hour of the morning, then? And wasn't that the tail end of Max's dressing gown I saw disappearing indoors? Don't tell me you're both up for a breath of fresh air this early?'

I shrugged. 'It's just, well, some of the paintings I want to sell ended up all over the courtyard floor during the night.' I hesitated. 'Max thinks it was a dog.'

She walked up to the van and peered in at its windows. Then she laughed. 'I expect he's right,' she said cheerfully. 'But at least it's gone now. So how about a bite of breakfast? And you can tell me, how is your mother these days?'

She bustled in, and I followed, telling her as humorously as I could of my mother's latest escapade with a good-looking Italian waiter. She laughed as she whisked around her kitchen, conjuring up as if by magic a breakfast fit for a king. But when I glanced up from my plate she was staring out of the kitchen window at the courtyard where my van stood. And she was frowning.

Later that morning Max reappeared, and showed me the old barn I was to use for my workshop. By then I had pulled myself together. There were times, I had decided, when I had too much of my mother in me. This was no time for letting my wayward emotions take over. Better by far to concentrate on the challenge of earning my inheritance, and the fact that Max so obviously doubted my ability merely served to stiffen my resolve.

'Will this do?' He looked around the barn with a critical eye. It was a bit dusty, with the remains of some machinery in one corner, but it was dry. There was a kind of half loft, with a ladder leading up to it, and a skylight which let in just about sufficient light. Luckily there was also electricity laid on. All in all, I couldn't have hoped for more. Max took my agreement for granted. 'I'll help you to bring in your equipment.'

I was glad of his assistance, and as we worked together, setting up my work-bench and mitre-saw, and bringing in rolls of canvases and the uncut framing, I gradually became more at ease. I even stole the odd surreptitious glance at him, studying the difference that time had made.

He was still lean and rangy, but his shoulders had broadened and there was new strength in his wiry frame. His face, too, had hardened, or perhaps that was not quite the right word. The jawline was more defined; the lips firmer; the forehead, under the hair that flopped forward as he bent to lift my

56

tools, had the trace of lines.

What had brought those about? I wondered. Seven years was a long time, and I had very little idea of what had happened to any of the Laceys since I left, only what the solicitor had told me, and the gossip my mother had been able to glean through her mysterious family grapevine. They were probably all quite changed. As I was myself, of course.

'Dreaming, Penny?' I came to myself with a start, and found Max lolling against the doorframe, regarding me with a slight smile hovering around that mobile mouth.

'I was merely thinking about the paintings,' I answered coldly. I hesitated, a little scared of laying myself open to his sarcasm, and then decided to take the risk. 'What d'you think of these, and these?'

I undid one of the rolls of canvases, and spread them out on an old pasting table I had found and pressed into service. I was proud of my choice of pictures. Any home, I felt, would be graced by them, landscapes that glowed with autumn colours, street scenes that fairly bustled with life, seascapes that brought with them the tang of salt and the roar of the waves and all within the range of the ordinary man-in-the-street.

Max peered from behind me, his arm heavy across my shoulder. I tried to ignore it, knowing the gesture to be a completely natural and friendly one. I was glad of it, for it showed perhaps that his initial suspicion of me had faded, but that was all it meant. But it was no use, I felt heat rising inside me like a tide, and on the pretext of showing him more paintings, I moved away from his casual embrace.

'You're right,' he said at last. 'They're good. Really good.' He turned apologetically. 'I should have trusted your good taste, Penny. You always had a flair. I should have known.'

'Thank you,' I said, both relieved and gratified. Afraid that I was grinning foolishly with pleasure, I rushed on.

'And the stall, Max? You promised to show me that.'

'Oh, of course. It's up here. Just a sec, I'll get it down.'

Max climbed the ladder into the loft, and came down with his arms filled with dusty canvas and laths. I helped him, and together we laid it out.

'It's awfully heavy,' I said doubtfully. 'I'll never manage to put the thing up . . . never in a month of Sundays.'

A voice broke in. 'We'll help you, won't we, Margaret?'

Brian and his sister were standing in the doorway, peering into the barn. He was smiling with easy good humour, and Margaret stood behind him, tall and elegant in a pale blue two-piece. She looked over his shoulder and twittered. 'Of course, but d'you think you'll like doing this, Penny? It just doesn't seem to be you somehow. I wonder . . .'

And I wondered. I wondered how a woman as ineffectual as Margaret had successfully made and sold garden gnomes. There must be a lot more to her than I had imagined.

'She'll manage,' Max said rather grimly.

'Of course she will,' Brian enthused. 'We'll all give a hand.'

To my surprise, for all Brian and Margaret's kindness, I found myself resenting their assumption that I could only make out if the Laceys took me in hand. I preferred Max's dry assertion that I would find my own way out of any mess I found myself in.

'I've managed on my own up until now,' I said pointedly, 'I've had to.' And then, realising that sounded ungracious, and feeling genuinely touched by their desire to help, I relented with a smile. 'But it's kind of you to offer.'

Margaret scurried forward and took my arm, hugging it to her. 'We're looking forward to it,' she said breathlessly, 'truly, Penny. It reminds me of the time I worked the stall, before — before — Howard died.' She broke off and fished in her pocket for a dainty lace handkerchief.

She had no need to say more, and it made me feel an ungrateful pig. How would I feel if I had lost my husband, and then found my inheritance handed on a plate to somebody else, not, I suspected, as magnanimous as Margaret.

'It's sweet of you,' I said, and I meant it.

It was lunchtime by then, and we made a family occasion of it. Brian and Margaret were cheerful, and appeared to be genuinely interested in my plans. I didn't mention the events of the night before to them. I was beginning to think that Max must have been right and I may have carelessly left the van door ajar. It was either that, or return to my original suspicion that Max was responsible, and somehow I did not want to do that.

I didn't have a lot of time to ponder such questions, because — in typical Lacey manner — they all decided that there was no time like the present for introducing me to the market, and getting the stall set up. The pitch had, it appeared, been booked for a long time. All it needed was for me to get going.

If I did feel a little nervous, I hid the fact. I would rather have stayed at Lacey Manor on my own, quietly framing my pictures and building up my stock . . . but it was not to be. I was swept along by Brian and Margaret's enthusiastic organisation, and I did not have enough strength of character to shout, 'Whoa!' At least they were making it clear that they wanted me to be a success. I wasn't so sure about Max, though. I couldn't decide what he wanted.

Throughout lunch he was very quiet, and when we left the dining room and abandoned the dishes to Mrs Mac-Donald, he took me to one side.

'You don't have to go today, you know.'

I flushed. Was I that obvious, or did he have his own devious reasons for delaying my introduction to the market?

'But I want to,' I assured him airily. 'The sooner I get the stall set up, the better. And since Brian is free today to help with it, and since Margaret has been so kind as to — '

'All right. You don't need to protest any further — I get the picture, if you'll excuse the pun.' He looked at me darkly for a moment, and then shrugged. 'Might as well get on with it, I suppose.'

We were held up for a little while because Margaret needed to pop back to her house to change her clothes, the elegant two-piece not being quite the thing for what we had in mind. Max decided to load all the gear for the stall into his large utility vehicle. He made it clear that he preferred to do this on his own, and so Brian and I had a quiet stroll around the grounds of Lacey Manor. We wandered, by mutual consent, along the paths we had taken when I was but a child, and leaned against the five-barred gate I used to straddle then. It quite took me back to the old days, and I told him so.

'Ah, yes, the good old days,' he agreed. 'But one can't go back, you know, Penny.'

For Brian, he sounded surprisingly serious, and I looked at him in surprise. He saw my glance, and grinned.

'Things were easier when you were young, don't you think?' he murmured. 'Everything cut and dried. No responsibilities. No problems.'

'Do you have problems then, Brian?' I asked with interest. 'I thought the Lacey Pottery was a highly successful firm.'

He hesitated. Then, seeming to make up his mind, he shrugged and laughed. 'Oh, yes, it is. Pay no attention to me, Penny dear, I'm just getting maudlin.

We returned to the courtyard, and waited in silence until Max had finished loading. I had plenty to think about. Brian had been right — you could not return to the way things were in the past. Circumstances changed. Think of poor Margaret, her husband dying so young, leaving her with two small children. And Brian, too. I had the niggling feeling that perhaps inheriting the factory had not been quite the windfall I had supposed it to be. In which case, what did he really think about my inheriting Great-aunt Penelope's money?

Was this what Max had been hinting at when he had turned on me in fury, the evening I arrived? 'You really don't know anything,' he had said. I was beginning to think that was true.

* * *

'There,' Max said with satisfaction, as he slammed shut the door of the Ute. 'We're all packed up and ready to go. I take it you don't want to start trading today, Penny?'

'Oh, no!' I was startled. I wasn't ready to jump into such an enterprise yet. I needed to dip my toe in the water first, so to speak. I had to learn a lot more about it. Perhaps Margaret would teach me. After all, she had done it in the past, and obviously wanted to help. Perhaps giving me a hand would take her mind off her own troubles.

The object of my thoughts came strolling along the drive. 'I didn't hold you up, I hope?' She smiled.

I assured her that I didn't mind. We were in no real hurry, and the time she had taken had been justified. Even though she now wore trousers and a plaid shirt, she still looked well groomed, her hair shining, her make-up flawless. Her clothes were expensive — even I could see that — and I wondered rather guiltily whether she would be able to manage to dress with quite such a disregard to money in the future. Two small boys to rear — and no money from Penelope — it would be no easy task. I resolved once more to talk to her about it, and see what we could do. After all, though I could hardly remember her children, they *were* my blood relations too, and as such I could surely be allowed to take a hand in paying for their education.

'Let's be on our way,' Max said.

He took his place in the driving seat, and Brian got in at the back with Margaret, leaving the passenger seat for me. I was just about to climb in, when Mrs MacDonald called from the kitchen door.

'Miss Penny, dear, could I just have a word with you about dinner?'

'Of course.' I turned to Max. 'I won't be a sec.'

As I walked over to Mrs MacDonald, it occurred to me uncomfortably that she should not be asking my instructions. I might have inherited Great-aunt's money, but the house was Max's, and as such she should still take her instructions from him. I wondered how to put this tactfully to her.

'About dinner — ' I began, as I reached her.

She stopped me, with her hand on my arm, and drew me into the doorway out of earshot of the others. 'I don't want to talk about food,' she murmured, a bright smile belying the worry in her eyes.

'Then what . . . ?'

'Just be careful, Penny dear,' she muttered. 'Just be careful.'

I was taken aback. 'But what d'you mean? I'm not driving. And Max *is* careful, you know that.'

She pursed her lips, as though dubious of what to say. 'Just remember — things aren't always what they seem,' she said shortly. 'That's all.'

She gave me a little push. 'Off with you now,' she continued loudly and brightly. 'And lobster salad it will be. I thought I was right in thinking that one of your favourites. Have a nice afternoon, all of you.'

I waved back at her, and took my place in the car. Max already had the engine running, and I realised that there was no way that any of them could have heard the strange conversation.

'We're off,' Margaret said happily. 'Aren't you excited, Penny?'

'I'll say,' I answered with enthusiasm. But that wasn't the end of it. I was also puzzled, and just a bit apprehensive. What had Mrs MacDonald meant? What did I have to be careful about?

I glanced sideways at Max's stern visage as he kept his eyes on the road, his strong hands lightly clasping the steering-wheel. Was Max all that he seemed? Was that what Mrs Mac-Donald had been warning?

I felt a strange prickle up my spine, but dismissed it angrily. Mrs Mac-Donald was just being over cautious — probably remembering the happen-ings of all those years ago, and imagining that I still held a torch for Max Lacey.

That was it. She didn't want me getting hurt again. I settled in the car seat and watched the scenery sliding by. Well — there was no possibility of that.

So, there was nothing to worry about. Was there?

4

The market was a revelation to me. I had not expected quite so much bustle, such colour, such life, such noise.

The stalls were packed together, contraptions of struts and canvas, some striped, some plain. And each stall was different. Everything was sold there, candy floss and toffee apples, children's wear, anoraks, garden produce and bric-a-brac. We pushed our way through, Max leading, not looking around to see if I was following. Margaret, taking pity on me, stuck by my side breathlessly explaining and enlarging on what we saw. Brian solidly brought up the rear.

Apart from the ordinary stalls there were large open vans, from which people were selling to their near-hypnotised audiences. I stopped in front of one, where a young man was selling towels. He had tousled sun-bleached hair and square-jawed face. His shoulders were well-muscled, brown skin constrasting with his faded blue jersey, and his hips slender in their tight denim jeans. He held the crowd in the palm of his hand, with smiling good-humoured banter flowing fast and furious. He appeared to be enjoying himself so hugely that I found myself wanting to buy from him. He held up a huge pink bath sheet.

'In your high street shops, this would cost sixteen pounds.' Confidently he surveyed the upturned faces of the crowd. 'But I'm not going to ask sixteen, am I? No . . . not fourteen. Not twelve.'

He caught my eye, and grinned at me. 'Lady, would you say this was good value at ten pounds.'

'I — er — yes, I suppose so.'

'Of course you would.' He came to the edge of his platform and spoke directly to me. His eyes were an amazing shade of blue.

'I can see you're a lady who knows what's what. But I won't charge ten — not eight — not six. Five pounds to the first person whose hand goes up.'

A forest of hands shot in the air, mine included. The stall-holder became busy handing out towels aided by an older man who took the money. Max — who by some instinct had realised I was no longer following him — caught hold of my arm and dragged me out of it.

'I thought for a minute you were going to buy all his stock,' he grumbled.

'Heavens,' I gasped. 'That was high-powered. I reckon he could sell anything to anybody.' I looked anxiously at my companions. 'I won't have to do that, will I?'

'Certainly not!' Margaret said with what could almost be called a snort. 'Your trade will be quite different.' The assumption of Lacey superiority again — even though I was not quite one of them.

'Mind you,' Brian said genially, 'It

would help if you could have a spiel of some sort.'

'A what?'

'A line of banter — sales talk,' Max explained. 'Look, Brian, don't confuse the girl yet. Just let's get the stall up. Here's our space.'

It was a small area, not far from the towel and bed linen van, and jammed between a little man demonstrating a vegetable chopping gadget, and a stall selling home-made cakes. Margaret and I bought some of the latter, while Max and Brian went off, to return later pushing their way with some difficulty through the crowd, carrying the equipment.

'It should really have been erected first thing,' Max grumbled. 'They don't like you putting stalls up once the market is open.'

'Well, now you tell me,' I muttered. 'Whose idea was it to come today, anyway? Not mine!'

'But it's for your benefit.'

As if I needed reminding. They were

all being so helpful — even Max. And yet underneath it all, I felt uneasy. The trouble was, I couldn't see why they were being so nice to me. Would I have been so obliging, in the circumstances? I'd like to think I would — but I was not sure. And again — I was not much use there, I could see that. All of the others knew what they were doing, and I had to stand helplessly by while they made sense of wood and canvas and pieces of rope, until almost by magic a stall took shape.

'Have you thought how you're going to display your paintings?' Brian asked. 'You can't just pin them to the sides.'

'Perhaps she could just pile them on the table,' Margaret added.

Were they mocking me? I might not know anything about it, but I did have commonsense.

'A framework of battens,' I said tersely. 'I'll knock them up this evening. I know exactly how I'm going to do it, but first I'll take some measurements.'

While I was doing that Margaret

grew bored, and wandered off to look at children's shoes. Brian bumped into an old friend, and stood chatting with him. And Max followed my every move with interest in those dark grey eyes.

'You'll need a money pouch,' he said. 'To fasten to your belt. It'll let you have your hands free, and keep your takings safe — '

'I know,' I interrupted impatiently. 'I've thought of all that. I bought one. *And* quantities of small change. *And* advertising material with my name and phone number on it.'

'My, my,' he quipped. 'You *have* been doing your homework!'

I gave him a suspicious look, but he smiled back blandly. He wiped his hair from his eyes. 'See the weights attached to these ropes? They're to keep the canvas down. You'll need them on a windy day. I'll fix them securely for you.'

He soon became busy, and I found myself in the way, having to skip out of his road now and again while he worked, engrossed, whistling between his teeth. It had always been a habit of his, I remembered, and the memory sent a quick shaft of pain through me. How far removed we were from those early days when I followed him around with blind adoration. Well — I knew better now!

'Ah, the lady who didn't want my towels!'

I whirled around to find myself looking into the laughing blue eyes of the man from the linen stall.

'Oh, it's you! What are you doing here?' I exclaimed, and then blushed at sounding so gauche. He'd taken me by surprise, and close up his charisma was even stronger. It was quite unnerving.

He grinned cheekily. 'Looking for you — what else?'

I was recovering quickly. 'I find that hard to believe,' I retorted with a smile. 'You had no idea that I would be here. And who's minding your van while you come looking for me?'

'My mate, Bert.' Suddenly he thrust

out a hand. 'I'm Pete Barlow. I heard about you setting up business here, so I thought I'd introduce myself, seeing we'll be neighbours, so to speak.'

News travelled fast in the market, I could see. I shook his hand. It was firm and warm, and held mine a fraction too long. It was not a disagreeable sensation, I pretended not to notice.

'Penelope Rossi.' I turned and introduced Max. 'My cousin, Max Lacey.'

Max glanced up and gave a brief nod. 'We've met before, I believe.'

Pete nodded. 'That's right — some time ago now, when you were selling — spare parts, wasn't it.'

He didn't really wait for Max to reply, but turned to me again. 'Seein' you don't seem very busy at the moment, why don't I show you around a bit. Introduce you to people — you know. It'll all help.'

Well — why not? I was under no illusions as to Pete's type. His admiring glances were, if anything, somewhat too obvious; his manner a little too overpowering. But, all the same, he was an extremely attractive man, and it was doing my ego a power of good. And my ego needed it. It had taken quite a bashing recently, what with finding out that Simon was more concerned with my inheritance than my well-being, and discovering that Max still held the poor opinion of me that he had acquired all those years ago. Yes, it would be nice to let Max see that somebody appreciated me.

'I'd love to,' I said.

He took my arm, and we moved away, joining the stream of shoppers. I looked back and saw Max standing glaring after us, a scowl on his dark face. Serve him right, I thought with satisfaction!

As it turned out, my guided tour was interesting. Pete knew everybody, and it was quite amusing to see the glances our progress aroused — speculation on the part of the men, and more than a few glances of jealously from some of the women. I could not have had a better guide. I found myself chatting to many of the stall holders, and without the Lacey family breathing down my neck, I felt more at ease. Perhaps working here was not going to be too bad after all.

We approached a fast-food stall. Pete stopped and bought two hot dogs, fat with onions, and I clutched mine in its white paper bag and wiped away the grease that trickled down my chin.

'Why are you doin' this?' he asked suddenly.

I must have looked surprised — perhaps even a little annoyed — because he frowned. 'I mean — a classy bird like you. Are you one of the Lacey breed? Doin' it for kicks, are you? Want to see how the other half live . . ?'

'Is that how you see the Laceys?' I asked with interest. It had never occurred to me to wonder what other people made of Great-aunt Penelope's experiments with her grandchildren's lives.

Pete shrugged. 'Stands to reason — just look at 'em. Public school types — and then they start working the market. But they don't stay, do they? Not like we have to.' Crumpling his now empty paper bag into a ball, he threw it into a nearby litter bin, and fished out a handkerchief to wipe his hands. 'No — ' he went on. 'Next thing is, they've got businesses of their own, making money hand over fist. At least that Max Lacey is. And I hear his brother owns the pottery now.'

'They've worked very hard for what they have,' I protested. 'Max built up the business all on his own — ' I stopped, wondering what I was doing defending Max's good name to a man I hardly knew.

'And you . . ?' Pete slipped his hand under my elbow, and turned me towards him. Gently he wiped my chin with his handkerchief. 'Messy girl,' he murmured, and then — 'why are you doing it? Slumming?'

'No, I am *not!*' I said indignantly, and

before I knew what I was doing, I found myself telling him all about it. He listened to me with flattering attention, and while I was talking we moved on, and it seemed quite natural that Pete's arm should be around my waist, steadying me through the buffeting crowds.

'So you see . . . ' I concluded triumphantly. 'I *need* to make a success of my stall, or else I stand to lose everything.'

He frowned, his eyes drooping a little. It gave him a hooded appearance, suddenly at odds with his usual cheery manner. 'They won't let you — you know?'

'What — what d'you mean?' I faltered.

He gave a bitter little laugh. 'Can't you see. As plain as the nose on . . . on Bert's face. If you make out here, the Lacey's lose everything — '

'Not everything,' I objected.

'Damn near,' he insisted. 'They're not going to let you walk away with the bulk of your great-aunt's fortune. Not the great nose-in-the-air Laceys.'

'You're quite wrong about them,' I argued. 'They might have resented me a bit — but they are all being extremely helpful. I don't know what bee you may have in your bonnet about the Laceys being snobbish, but they're not really. And . . . ' I went on, feeling somehow that I had to vindicate myself, 'I can assure you, I'm not one of them.'

'I'm glad to hear it.' He was laughing again, the blue eyes that looked down into mine were twinkling. We came to a halt in front of a dog-food stall, and he let go of my waist and took both of my hands in his.

'All right — I'll lay off the criticism of your relatives, since you're so touchy. But as to you being different . . . then prove it, Miss Penelope Rossi.'

I was puzzled. 'Prove it — but how?'

'By havin' dinner with me tonight, of course.'

'Oh!'

He had caught me neatly. I was not

certain that I wanted to have dinner with Pete Barlow, pleasant company though he was. Not sure whether I wanted to — and not sure what Max would think. That thought made me stiffen. What should it matter *what* Max thought? I was my own woman, and could do what I liked. And if I refused Pete he would only be confirmed in his poor opinion of the Laceys, and of me in particular . . .

'Very well.' I nodded. 'I'd like that, Pete.'

We continued our stroll, working our way around the market in a circle, until we arrived back at my stall. Max seemed to have deserted it, there was nobody there. I wondered what I was supposed to do now.

'They seem to have scarpered,' Pete said.

'They'll be back for me,' I insisted.

'Well — I'd better be getting back. Bert'll be giving me hell for being away so long.'

I suspected he would, and I bet it

would not be for the first time, either

'Are you sure you'll be all right?' he asked.

I held out my hand. 'Positive, and thanks for the guided tour, Pete. I'll see you tonight.'

He nodded and smiled, vivid blue eyes holding mine. 'Seven-thirty do you? I'll pick you up.'

Then he was off, back to his own pitch, and I was left all alone. I felt like a fish out of water, standing there beside an empty stall, and I began to feel anger rise. Why had Max abandoned me like this? Was he just trying to make me feel awkward?

It was with a sigh of relief that I saw Margaret's fair head amongst the crowd, and realised that she was making her way back to me.

'Ah, *there* you are,' she said a little sharply. 'We're all waiting to go home Max is furious with you.'

'With me?' I could feel a flush rising in my cheeks. 'Why should Max be angry with me?'

She gave a little smile, and a conciliatory pat on my arm. 'He didn't say. You know Max, he doesn't say much — but one can always tell. Well — ' she said, with a return to her usual breathless manner. 'You did rather leave him in the lurch, to do all the work — now, didn't you?' She looked at me and gave a funny little shrug. 'It can't be easy for you, Penny. If — well, if ever you need somebody to talk to, you know I'll always be willing to listen.'

She flushed, as though embarrassed by her sudden outburst of friendliness. It was out of character for her, and must have cost her quite a bit to go against her 'stiff upper lip' British reserve. I have not inherited that particular trait, and there and then in the middle of the market, I hugged her.

'I'll remember that, Margaret. Thanks.'

She turned, but I put my hand out to stop her. 'Margaret,' I said quietly, not wanting the whole world to hear, 'I've been meaning to say to you — you don't have to worry. About the boys' school I mean. When I get the money, *if* I get the money, I'll see to all that. I think it's the least I can do.'

Her pale face was suffused with pink, and then just as quickly drained again, and her eyes filled with tears. 'That's — that's — well — that's just like you, Penny!' She gave a helpless little laugh. 'What can I say?'

'You don't need to say anything,' I told her briskly, knowing her dislike of emotion. 'Just lead the way to the car. We'd better get back.'

She set off without another word, and I followed her, seething at Max. He knew very well that there was nothing I could have done at the stall. I hadn't been needed, and there was no reason for me to feel guilty about exploring with Pete. If Max thought I was going to be apologetic, he had another think coming!

Brian was leaning against the car

when we arrived. He merely acknowledged my presence with a genial wave of the hand, and climbed into the back seat. Once more Margaret joined him at the rear, and I took my place beside Max. He said nothing — all the way back to Lacey Court.

I explained to Mrs MacDonald that I would be out to dinner, and apologised for any inconvenience caused. To my relief she looked pleased, and I wondered again about her cryptic comments earlier in the day, but since she did not elaborate on them I somehow did not feel able to bring the matter up. I spent the rest of the afternoon alone in the barn, framing more pictures, and knocking together the framework I knew I would need. I was quite happy to be by myself; I always found working with my hands therapeutic. Sawing and hammering kept me busy, and stopped some of the uncomfortable thoughts that had been bothering me, so I was not all that pleased when Max finally did put in an appearance.

He examined my work, testing it for strength, examining the joints. 'Yes . . . that should be just the job.'

'Glad you approve,' I said, somewhat tartly.

'Penny — ' He paused, and then pressed on. 'Penny, let's not be prickly with one another. I want you to succeed. I really do. Friends?'

I whirled around. 'It wasn't me who — ' Then I melted. I shouldn't have, but I did; he had that kind of effect on me. 'Friends,' I echoed weakly.

Somehow I found myself in his arms. Not swept in passionately, just . . . somehow gathered in, close to him. His cheek was pressed against my hair, and I could feel the warmth of him against me, could smell the familiar aroma of tweed, and aftershave.

I closed my eyes, and made no effort to draw away. Gone were the years that had passed, gone all my painstakingly acquired self-confidence, my shell of self-sufficiency. Achingly I admitted to myself that my schoolgirl crush on Max showed no sign of having abated. Rather had this further meeting forced it to change — to grow — to blossom, against my will, into something much deeper.

I didn't know whether I could handle it.

After the friendly hug, he released me, smiling down on me, those dear familiar laughter lines around his eyes, deepening. 'So — in that case, Penny, my dear, to prove that we are indeed old friends again, what say I take you out tonight? There's a nice old inn just this side of Malvern, I think you'd like it, and — '

'Oh Max,' I burst in, dismayed. 'I'm sorry — but I'm — well, I already have something lined up for tonight.'

'Oh.' For a moment he looked taken aback, his smile fading. Then he grinned, and shrugged. 'Sorry. I was taking too much for granted. I didn't realise you had any friends around here.'

'I don't. Well — ' Somehow I found it difficult to explain, but explain I must, because he would see Pete when he arrived to collect me later in the evening. 'I promised to have dinner with Pete Barlow.'

His eyebrows shot up. 'Pete from the market?' He sounded incredulous.

I tilted my chin defiantly. 'And why not?'

His laugh was abrupt. 'Oh, no reason at all, my dear. I should have guessed. You only met him for a few minutes — but then, perhaps you haven't changed as much as I thought you had. It wouldn't take long for you — '

'Oh, you pig!'

Furious I picked up the nearest thing to hand, which happened to be a hefty chunk of wood, but before I could even think what I intended to do with it, he had caught my arm in a vice-like grip, and I dropped it again. He couldn't stop my tongue though.

'You're just a snob, Max Lacey. That's all. Pete was right, you just play

90

at the market — slumming, as he put it. Well, I think you're nothing but a — parasite! Pete Barlow might not have been to university, but he is doing an honest job, and I think he's worth ten of you, and — and — '

He shook me until my teeth rattled. 'Don't be a silly little fool,' he grated. 'I care nothing about where the man went to school — or even whether he ever did. But I do care that you're going out with a man you know nothing about. Two minutes with him, and off you go. He has a reputation, you know.'

'I'm only going to dinner with him,' I gasped. 'Not joining his harem.' I gathered together all the defiance I could muster. 'And anyway, what business is it of yours, may I ask? I'm old enough to do whatever I please. And to date whoever I please.'

'And as many men as you want to — ' he stated.

This time I was too quick with him. He had forgotten that I was just as handy with my left hand, as my right.

Without a second's thought I slapped him, right across his face.

His head jerked back, and I stared, appalled at the blazing anger in his eyes.

'Max — ' I quavered, but I didn't finish my sentence; my surroundings were blotted out as his arms crushed me, his face swooped down, and his lips found mine.

The world spun. It was instinctive on his part, the brutal response of a man who thinks he has been pushed too far by a woman. He was punishing me, I knew, and yet I couldn't help it — I found myself returning his kiss. My arms, of their own volition, twined around his neck. My body pressed against him, wanting him, needing him, desperate to keep him long enough for his embrace to turn into the real thing — to mean that he loved me —

But he pushed me away.

'My God,' he exploded. 'You just can't help yourself, can you? Don't you know what you do to a man.'

I could feel hot tears spring into my eyes, my hands reaching out to him. 'But, Max — '

'Oh . . . forget it!' He turned on his heel, and stomped out of the barn, slamming the door so hard that I thought it would come off its hinges.

I sat on a stool and bawled like a baby. Why had I ever come back to Lacey Court? I wished fervently that Great-aunt Penelope had never written my inheritance into her will. Wished I had never seen Max Lacey again — I was happy enough, without him. Or thought I was. Now I knew better. I loved him. And life held nothing but misery for me every moment that he was near.

5

By the time Pete was due to arrive I'd dried my tears, showered and made myself presentable. More than that; out of sheer defiance I'd put on a clinging dress of green silk that perhaps was slightly more revealing than was good for it — or for me — and a pair of matching shoes, high-heeled enough to show off my legs to advantage. Then I'd swept my rebellious black curls into a frothy mass on top of my head, letting a few tendrils escape to give a fashionably dishevelled look, and disguised my reddened eyes with eyeliner and mascara. The effect was dramatic, as I could tell by Max's impression when I encountered him in the hall, on my way into the drawing-room.

I gave him a stiff little nod, and swept past, thinking that he would go on his way, but he followed me in.

'Penny . . . ' he began stiffly.

'I don't think we have anything to say to one another,' I said stiffly.

'But I *do* have something to say,' he rejoined with equal formality. 'I do wish to apologise.'

That I had not been expecting. A Lacey apologise! The sky would fall in next.

I shrugged. 'There's no need.' I wandered across to the old stone fireplace and leaned against the mantel, fiddling with one of the ornaments. I couldn't look Max in the eyes. If I did, he would surely be able to read my thoughts, and that would never do. I could only feign indifference, and find some way to get out of this house at the earliest opportunity.

'I think there is,' he insisted. 'I behaved badly. I can assure you. It won't happen again.'

There was a bitter note in his voice, as if he would as soon kiss a viper as kiss me. Well, he needn't worry. I was not going to ask him to. I told myself that I was well rid of any kind of relationship with Max Lacey, even friendship. But the thought only left me feeling empty and cold.

I was saved from having to reply by a knock at the door. Thankfully I left Max standing there, and walked into the hall. Mrs MacDonald had answered the door, but when she saw me she merely beckoned Pete inside, and turned to go back to the kitchen. Pete held out a small bunch of flowers, his eyes devouring me.

'Wow!' was all he said.

I wondered uneasily whether I had overdone things. 'Will I do?' I asked, genuinely wanting to know. 'I'm not overdressed or anything? Because if I am I can easily change. You didn't tell me where we were going, you see, and — '

'No, no — you're just fine.' He held out a hand. 'Princess, your carriage awaits you. I'll be the envy of everyone at the ball.'

'Fool!' I laughed, and gathered up my

jacket and handbag.

'Wait,' Pete said. 'Let me pin the flowers to your dress.'

The small corsage was already supplied with a fastener, and I stood compliantly while Pete pinned it on, standing intimately close to me. 'Your dress is the colour of the leaves,' he murmured, gazing into my eyes. 'I must have known.'

Max had followed me. He gave us both a look of pure contempt. 'Enjoy yourselves.'

'Thank you, Max,' I said icily. 'I am *sure* we shall.'

Pete's eyes missed nothing, and as we drove into the town he murmured, 'Sarcastic, your relative, isn't he?'

'Oh, that's just Max's way,' I said lamely, and then left it at that.

Heavy oak beams and firelight twinkling on polished brass and copper — your traditional old inn. Pete had made a reservation, and we were ushered to a booth, shielded from view by a high carved back, made comfortable by red velvet cushions. I did wonder whether this might be the very place Max had recommended, but pushed the thought from my mind.

To be honest, I felt a little awkward with Pete.

Coming hard on the heels of the scene with Max I was not feeling like small talk — much less like fending off a bit of a wolf. And that was what Pete was — I was experienced enough those days to know that. Charming, and fun — but not to be trusted with women. Max had not needed to warn me. But I was confident that I could handle Pete, and enjoy his company with no strings attached. I busied myself with the menu and then leaned back with a sigh of relief. Perhaps a night's relaxation was just what I needed.

He was quick to notice. 'Tired?' he asked.

I laughed. 'What have I to be tired about? I haven't even begun yet. Ask me tomorrow, after I've had a proper day at the market.'

'You'll be all right,' he said confidently, his eyes holding mine. 'Just smile at all the men, the way you're smiling at me, and they'll jump through hoops for you.'

I dropped my gaze. 'I suppose I should blush, kind sir,' I said lightly. 'But I don't have the complexion for it.' I picked up the menu. 'I'm starving,' I said fervently. 'Let's order, shall we?'

To my surprise I found that I was as hungry as I had described. Pete had certainly picked the right place, the food was delicious. Traditional English fayre at its best — roast beef with mouthwatering juices, baby carrots glistening with butter, peas, fresh from the pod, Yorkshire Pudding, light and fluffy.

And the wine, too — that was excellent. I had wondered what Pete would order, expecting that he might go for something pretentious — but instead we had a carafe of the house red — and it was good.

He reached across the table and

touched my hand. 'You know, Penny, this is really nice — I mean, it's quite a change for me.'

My eyebrows rose, and I laughed. That candid little boy butter-wouldn't-melt-in-the-mouth expression did not fool me. 'You mean — you never take a girl out for a meal? I find that hard to believe.'

His smile acknowledged his mistake. 'I mean — I seldom get the opportunity to take out anyone so beautiful — or so easy to talk to. You're something special. But of course you know that.'

Gently I withdrew my hand. 'I don't know anything of the sort. Wait until you see me tomorrow, after I've wrestled with my stock and stood on my feet for hours!'

He took the hint, and grinned — and bided his time. He was fun to talk to, provided I could stop him from getting too amorous. He was looking smart this evening, too. His hair had been trimmed, and he was wearing a well-cut suit and crisp white shirt, with a tie. His more formal clothes had not detracted from his sheer animal magnetism, though — and I knew I should handle him with care.

I found his stories of the market fascinating, and had no hesitation in picking his brains.

'People love sets of things,' he told me. 'Tie three cushions together, and they'll go for them — thinkin' they're getting a bargain. Sometimes they are, but often they're paying just the same. But they love it, see.'

I nodded, mentally scanning through my pictures. There were several small ones, suitable for bedrooms, that could conveniently be sold in batches. I would have to bear that in mind.

'And 'specials',' he went on. ' 'Today's special bargain' that always fetches 'em. You need a board up. Write on it in big bold letters.'

Absentmindedly I tucked in to the fruit salad and cream, my mind busy planning.

'Hey,' he said suddenly. 'Come back

— you're miles away.'

I apologised. 'I guess I'm rather strung up about starting, Pete. I hope I'll be all right. I expect I will — once I begin.'

'You'll have me nearby,' he said. 'So you'll have a friend in camp, so to speak.'

'I'll be glad of that,' I replied.

'You'll need it!'

I was dismayed. 'Will it be that bad?'

He laughed. 'I don't mean the selling. I mean the Laceys. With them around you, you're going to need a friend. I wouldn't trust any of them an inch.'

'Oh, Pete!' I laughed. 'Now you are exaggerating. I shouldn't have told you about the inheritance. It's made you imagine all kinds of things that just aren't true.' I set about demolishing his suspicions. 'Max might be difficult, but he would never harm me. And Margaret has been really sweet. And then there's Brian — a real steady type, if ever there was one. He doesn't seem the least bit bothered about my getting the money. Why should he? He's doing very well out of the factory.'

Pete took a long drink of wine, and looked steadily at me over the rim of his glass. 'Not what I heard,' he said.

Uneasiness trickled through me. Was nothing what it seemed. Mrs Mac-Donald had hinted as much. 'What d'you mean?'

'I heard Brian Lacey is in queer street. Expensive flat. Expensive women. Too fond of the gee gees. And the factory has been laying off men left right and centre, so there's little help there.'

If that were so, he must have been banking on getting a share of Great-aunt Penelope's money to help him out of his difficulties. I shivered.

'Here,' said Pete. 'That's enough. You're getting down in the dumps. Let's go on, shall we? I know a great little night spot.'

Perhaps it would have been better to call it a night then and there, but I was too busy with the information Pete had given me to even think straight, and so I didn't argue, but followed him out of the restaurant and into his car.

The night spot was hardly 'great.' It *was* very dark, and expensive, and intimate. The couples on the tiny dance floor appeared to be glued together. Not the kind of place I would have chosen to visit with a virtual stranger. But there I was, so I had to put up with it. We had some more drinks, stronger than I expected, and my head began to feel muzzy.

'Dance?'

It was something to do. So I agreed. Pete was a good dancer, but dancing was not really on his mind. Gradually he pulled me closer and closer, until — like the rest of those dancing, we were merely swaying to the music. I tried to pull away, but he only tightened his grip. 'Relax,' he said smoothly. 'Enjoy yourself.'

It *had* been a mistake to go out with Pete until I knew him better, I realised that now. If I had stuck to a semi-professional relationship in the market, it would have been fine, but he was reading more into my acceptance of his invitation to a night out than I had ever intended.

I tried to look as though I was enjoying myself, but surreptitiously I kept glancing at my watch, and as soon as I decently could I decided that enough was enough.

'I've got to be up early,' I told him truthfully. 'I think perhaps it's time to leave.'

He did not demur. 'I'll get your jacket,' he said at once.

In his car I breathed a sigh of relief. The evening was over, or virtually so. It had been enjoyable — in parts. I leaned my head back against the seat, and shut my eyes. 'Thanks for the lovely evening, Pete,' I said sleepily. 'It's been fun.'

He dropped a hand on to my thigh, and patted it. 'My pleasure,' he purred. I put my own hand down, and firmly took hold of his. That seemed the best way to restrain any further wanderings without making a big issue of it. Then I must have dropped off to sleep.

★　★　★

'Wake up — we're here.'

I stretched and yawned. 'Oh — I'm sorry, I didn't realise how tired I was. Hey — wait a minute, this isn't Lacey Court.'

We were parked outside a small house in what appeared to be the suburbs. A light was burning in the porch. I turned to Pete with indignation. 'What on earth d'you think . . ?'

'I thought you'd like a coffee before setting off home.' Although it was dark I could hear the smile in his voice. He sounded casual, genuine. I hesitated.

'I share the house with Bert,' he explained. 'He'd love to meet you.'

I couldn't see my watch. 'But will he still be up?' I asked.

'Of course,' he said smoothly. 'Always waits up for me. A proper old hen, he is. Come along.'

'I really ought to be getting back.'

'One coffee, and I'll take you straight home. Promise.'

'Oh — very well then.'

As I got out of the car, the wind hit me. It had turned gusty and cold, and I shivered. Perhaps a hot cup of coffee would be nice.

The house was small, but neat and tidy. It sounded as though there was no woman looking after the two men, but the little lounge had a comfortable settee facing a large TV, and a print of Van Gogh's Sunflowers on the wall.

Pete crossed the room, turned on a bar of the electric fire and slid a compact disc into a stereo unit. Soft music began to play. He turned the lights down low. 'Make yourself comfortable, I won't be a sec.'

He disappeared into what I took to be the kitchen, and I looked around me. No sign of any Bert, I noticed. Well — he'd probably taken himself off to bed. As no doubt Pete knew he would have. I was beginning to feel that all this was part of a well-laid plan. Pete had better watch himself, or I'd get really cross.

'Two coffees coming up. Instant, I'm afraid.'

'That's fine.' In my relief, I gave Pete a dazzling smile. I had been thinking all kinds of things — letting my imagination run away with me, as usual. It was Max's fault, for putting ideas into my head. I moved up to let Pete sit beside me, and gratefully cupped my cold hands around the coffee.

'Tell me about yourself,' I said between sips. 'Have you worked the market stall all your life?'

It turned out that he had inherited it from his father. Market stalls seemed to run in families hereabouts! His old man had been something of a stick-in-the-mud, it seemed, and Pete was proud of the way he had increased the business.

'Psychology,' he explained. 'You have to know what gets the punter going, and then cash in. You can make them believe anything, once they want to buy. Psychology, that's what it is.'

Conning people, I would have called it, but perhaps that wasn't fair — the stuff he sold was not that bad, though not perhaps the quality that those buying it imagined. I finished my coffee and replaced the cup on the saucer. 'That was lovely, Pete — but now I have to go.'

He slid an arm around my shoulder. 'Oh, c'mon, Penny. No need to go yet — let yourself go a bit.'

So here we had it — the old come-on. Time to put an end to it, once and for all.

'And where's Bert?'

'He must have been tired, and gone to bed,' he said smoothly. 'Don't worry about him. He won't interrupt us.'

His other arm was creeping around my waist. I gave him a hefty push. 'You're dead right he won't, Pete, because there won't be anything to interrupt. Please take me home — right now!'

His smile hardened. 'C'mon, Pen. Don't give me that. You're not the kind of girl to be a shrinking violet. Anyone can see that. Let your hair down a bit.'

There it was again — my looks giving the wrong impression. What did I have to do to convince men that I was not a bit of 'all right?' Wear a veil maybe?

'I'm sorry, Pete,' I said coldly. 'I'm afraid you've jumped to the wrong conclusions. You asked me out for a meal. Well, we've had that. Now I want to go home.'

He chuckled. 'Playing hard to get, eh?' He leaned over me, forcing me backwards, mouth reaching for mine. Instinctively I shot my head forward, trying to thrust him off, and accidentally butted him, hard on the nose.

He swore, and backed away, and I took the opportunity to jump away from him, and gathered up my belongings. Outwardly I was calm, but inside I was terrified. Now I'd angered him I would be no match for Pete if he used his superior strength.

'You little fool,' he bellowed. 'I'm just not good enough, is that it? Not after the precious Laceys. Just like the rest, you are. Nothing but a damned little snob.'

'You're talking a lot of nonsense,' I snapped. 'I'm sorry if I hurt you, but it was your own fault. Now I'm going. Goodnight, Pete, and thanks for a lovely night out!'

The last I saw of him he was desperately dragging a handkerchief out of his pocket, to catch the blood that had started to drip from his nose. I dashed from the room, and out of the front door. I didn't know which way to go. I'd been asleep when we'd arrived — where would I find a taxi at this time of night? Where was the nearest phone box? It was dangerous to be wandering alone in the dark, and equally dangerous to stay dithering about where I was, if Pete came rushing out after me. Cursing my own stupidity, I began walking quickly — somewhere nearby, surely I would find a phone?

At first the only sound in the darkness was that of my high heels, clip-clopping along the pavement. It had begun to drizzle, and the wind was stronger now, buffeting me and tugging at my clothes. My carefully arranged hair slithered down, wet strands whipping across my face. I shivered, and buttoned my jacket up at the neck. Then I heard a car. As it reached me, it slowed down. I walked faster, and it picked up speed. In sudden panic I kicked off my shoes and began to run, only vaguely aware of the cold pavements and the puddles I was splashing through. I dodged down the next turning to the left — then scurried across the road to take the next one to the right. The car kept pace, then overtook me.

A window wound down. 'Get in!'

I gave a whimper of terror and, like a petrified rabbit, turned to run back the way I had come. The voice came again. 'Penny, for goodness' sake, stop messing about and get in the car.'

'Max!'

As I stood there, frozen with relief, Max got out and bundled me into the passenger seat. 'Stay there a moment,' he said grimly, and then slammed the door. I sat huddled and miserable, thankful for the quiet warmth of the car's interior. Minutes later Max got in and dumped my shoes in my lap. He drove in silence.

At first all I could think of was what a fool I had been, and how stupid I must appear to him. From sheer reaction, I began to sniffle. Max handed me a handkerchief, and I blew my nose and dried my eyes and face. Then it occurred to me that Max could not have been there purely by chance. He must have been shadowing us all evening. How long had he sat there, outside Pete's house? What would he have thought if I had *not* come running out of it in such obvious distress? Been highly delighted, I thought sourly, to find that his poor opinion of me had been justified. I wished he would say something — anything.

At last, just as we turned into the drive of Lacey Court, I broke the silence. 'How — did you know I was at Pete's?' I asked in a small voice. 'Were you following me?'

He drew up in the courtyard, and turned off the engine. 'Just as well I was,' he said witheringly. 'What went on in there, Penny? I think you'd better tell me.'

'Nothing!' I bit my lip. 'It's true, Max. Pete just asked me in for coffee.'

'And you went. Just like that. A man you hardly knew. Are you stupid, Penny? To go into a house alone with him.'

'No! I didn't,' I insisted. 'He said he shared with Bert. You remember — that rather nice older man he works with. He said Bert would be waiting up to meet me. I didn't think there was any harm.'

He got out of the car and slammed his door viciously, stomping off to the house, leaving me to follow. Muttering under my breath I pushed my feet into my shoes, and raced head down through the wind and rain after him. I caught him up in the kitchen.

'Max, you've got to listen to me. Honestly, I didn't think Pete would behave like that.'

He pounced on that. 'Like what? What did he do, Penny?'

'Nothing. Nothing really.'

He snorted. 'And you came racing out like that because of nothing?'

'Well — he was just getting a bit fresh. But I could handle that. It was when I made his nose bleed that I . . . '

'You did what?'

To my surprise, he began to laugh.

'I didn't mean to,' I said a bit huffily. 'I'm sure he was going to drive me home. I don't think I was in any real danger, so don't expect me to be grateful to you.'

'Oh, I won't,' he said sarcastically. 'That's the last thing I'd expect from you, Penny. Now go upstairs and get out of those wet clothes. Bed is the best place for you. You do have to work tomorrow, remember?'

Yes, I remembered, and I was not much looking forward to it. Not now. Wearily I turned to drag myself up the stairs. As I went Max could not refrain from a parting shot. 'Pete Barlow has a reputation, you know. I did warn you, Penny.'

'Get lost!' I retorted inelegantly. Then, thinking of something even more telling to say, I stopped at the turn of the stairs and looked down at him. 'At least I enjoyed myself until then. That's more than I would have done if I'd taken you up on *your* invitation!'

The look of surprise and anger on his dark features should have pleased me, but somehow it didn't.

I had a quick shower, washed my hair and dried it, and then thankfully crawled into bed. I was bone-shakingly tired, but sleep eluded me. My mind was a jumble of pictures — the market — Pete and his towels — Brian, looking worried — my paintings — the stall

— Max, and the way I felt when I heard his voice in the darkness. Throughout it all the wind howled outside, and gusts rattled my bedroom window. Rain dashed against the glass. I had visions of starting my market trading in pouring rain. Batches of three. Three bedroom paintings; how much should I charge? Which ones should I put together; the flower paintings? What would Pete say if I saw him tomorrow? Why had I been so unnecessarily rude to Max? Max . . . Max.

At last I fell asleep.

'Penny. Penny, wake up!'

The thumping on my door woke me with a jolt. Bleary eyed I grabbed my alarm clock — five o'clock! What was he wanting?

'Penny, it's Max. Get up. We've got to go to the market.'

'At *this* hour?' I just couldn't believe it. I knew I had to be there early, but this was ridiculous. And what did Max mean by 'we?' He had a business to run, and I had not been expecting him to be watching over my shoulder on my first day. Crossly I rolled out of bed, and opened the door a fraction.

'What's the matter? It's too early. Go away.'

He hissed at me through the crack. 'The stall has been blown down. I've just had a phone call. If you want to start trading today we'll have to go now and put things right.'

What a good start! As I struggled into my jeans and sweater I wondered if they had all begun in this way. As Max drove me through the deserted streets he explained.

'One of the drivers who makes an early delivery of fruit and veg noticed it. He knew it was ours, so gave me a call. Just as well he did.'

'It *was* blowing awfully hard,' I said, stifling a yawn. 'A gale really, I suppose. Has there been much damage in the market?'

'No . . . oo,' he said thoughtfully. 'According to the driver ours is the only stall down.'

That woke me up. 'That's funny. If it was blowing that hard you'd expect more to be gone.'

'No use speculating until we see the damage.'

It was bad enough. The stall was flattened, the canvas in a heap on the ground, great puddles of rain collected in its folds. My heart sank, and I wished once more that I had not taken on this crazy enterprise.

'I can't understand it,' Max muttered. 'Why should your stall be the only one?'

'Perhaps you didn't fasten those ropes properly,' I suggested.

He shook his head. 'Look, Penny. They've been cut. And even then, only the canvas would have blown away. The whole stall has been tipped to one side.'

'Well — thank goodness it isn't raining now.' I took hold of one side of the framework. 'It's no use worrying why. I've got to get it all back together again.'

I was glad I had Max. I could never

have done it on my own. As it was, it was hard enough, and Max worked like fury. I helped as best I could, and after about an hour we had managed to re-erect it. Only then did I allow myself to wonder.

Somebody must have cut those ropes deliberately. But who? Uneasily, I remembered the fury on Pete's face when I had left him, clutching a hankie to his nose. Was this his way of getting his own back on me?

Max broke into my thoughts. 'Definitely sabotage. Any ideas?'

I shook my head. 'Kids, perhaps. Vandals?'

'On your stall only? That hardly seems likely.'

I didn't want to tell him of my suspicions. If I saw Pete I would judge for myself. I ran my hands through my hair. 'Well, how am I to know?' I answered Max. 'At least we've got it together again. There isn't time to think of the whys and wherefores. I've got to get back to collect my things, if I'm to trade at all today.'

Luckily he didn't press the issue, but drove me back to Lacey Court as fast as he could without breaking the speed limit — much! There he insisted that I should have something to eat before I set off again.

'D'you want me to come with you?' he asked.

I shook my head. 'No, Max. You've done enough. I've got the van loaded. I should be all right, and you have a business to run.'

He gave me a hurried peck on the cheek before he disappeared to tidy himself up before leaving for work. I also retired to my room to tidy up before setting off once more for the market.

I smiled to myself, remembering that chaste kiss on my cheek, contrasting it to Max's angry embrace of the night before. My smile faded. Max was somebody else who was angry with me. And someone who had a lot to gain if I gave up my claim to the inheritance.

How did I know where he had been while Pete and I had been eating our meal? He must have known we would be safely occupied for an hour or so. Or maybe after he brought me home? There had been plenty of time for him to slip out again then. Would I have heard if he had driven out into the wind and the rain? Somehow, I did not think so.

And Brian — was it true what Pete had hinted about his money problems. I would try to find out from Margaret.

Max — Pete — Brian. Could I trust any of them? Which one had deliberately set out to wreck my plans? Or was it all just coincidence. I only wished I knew.

6

The life of the market bustled around me, noisy and colourful, demanding and incessant.

'Eight pounds each the small flower paintings — three for twenty. A set'll look lovely on your bedroom wall.' I had soon discarded my natural nervousness, and was shouting my wares with the best of them. 'Three flower paintings for twenty pounds, prices marked on the bigger ones.'

'Mmm — I wonder?' The fat woman with the raffia shopping bag turned to her husband. 'What d'you think, Sidney?'

He scratched his head. 'You know these things better'n me, luv.'

I wasn't going to let this sale slip through my fingers. 'What's the colour scheme in your bedroom?'

'Well, the carpet's a sort of deep rose,

123

sort of. Then the walls are lilac, and the bedspread's pink; I thought those orange poppies might brighten it up.'

I winced as I nodded gravely. 'Here . . . I think these would suit you better.' I held up three small paintings of delicate sweet peas — all slightly different — in pale pink frames. If anything could fit into the maelstrom of colour she had indicated, these might. I told myself.

'I like them,' Sydney said, suddenly sure of himself.

That, apparently, did it. Notes changed hands and they went away highly pleased with themselves.

I was pleased, too. At least I had learned something useful from Pete last night, and it was paying dividends. I had sold four sets of small flower pictures already, and made a note that I must order more straightaway, to allow time for shipment from Hong Kong. As well as the flower paintings I'd sold a large gilt-framed painting reminiscent of The Hay Wain, and several other lesser ones — and it wasn't even lunch-time.

The woman from the cake stall nodded at me. 'You're catching on. 'Course, some days are better than others, you'll find. Still, you're not doing badly.'

I smiled at her, warmed by her words. That was the nicest thing about the market, the camaraderie of those working the stalls. It was like belonging to one huge family, competing, but willing to close ranks to look after their own. Above all, I would have shown Max that I could cope. His opinion meant more to me than anything else on earth. I could just imagine his dark grey eyes smiling, his mouth lifting at the corners. 'Well done,' he'd say. 'I knew you could do it.'

Well, maybe that was all wishful thinking. I didn't even know whether Max would be pleased or not. 'Nothing is as it seems, Mrs MacDonald had more or less told me, and that embraced all the Laceys, but most of all

Max. The strange thing was, I found it didn't make any difference. I still wanted Max to think well of me. If I couldn't have his love, at least I craved his approval.

My feet were aching, and in spite of it being a cold day, with the wind still blustery and chill, I felt hot in my anorak. I unzipped it and tucked it away under a trestle table. I shifted from one foot to the other, wishing I could sit down.

I had felt really awkward when I'd first arrived, but had been too busy fixing wires across the wooden battens to bother much about anybody else. I'd tried to display the paintings as invitingly as possible, but when my first customer stopped and began examining them critically, I had nearly died! I was in a blind panic, but luckily she had decided to buy, and that had given me confidence.

Since then the morning had worn on — sometimes slowly, and sometimes at a hectic pace. Customers, I found, came in batches — like double-decker buses when you're waiting at a bus stop — clustering together for reassurance. If a few people gathered around my stall, then inevitably others joined them. If one person decided to buy, I was more likely to make a sale to another.

I was learning fast, and one thing I was definitely finding out was how tiring it all was — but how exhilarating. Even if there had not been an inheritance at the end of it, I would be glad of this experience.

There was a short lull before the arrival of more prospective customers, and I used it to fetch pictures from my van to fill up the empty gaps left by those that had been sold. Greatly daring, I decided to try something a little more pricey. I'd commissioned a copy of Constable's Flatford Mill. It was good, and a popular subject, with the barge on the river, and the small boy perched on the tow horse, looking backward over his shoulder. In big letters I chalked up on a blackboard, *WHY PAY THOUSANDS WHEN YOU CAN HAVE YOUR OWN MASTERPIECE FOR ONLY £200?* Then in smaller letters I was careful to put, 'Copy of painting by J. S. Constable.' Not that anybody would surely be so foolish as to imagine they were getting the real thing for that price!

I judged it would be too much for the market — few people would be walking around with that much spare cash. But on the other hand it might bring forth enquiries, and I could invite customers to another exhibition in the barn. It was good value at the price, too — I had spent quite a bit on this one, cheap though the Hong Kong copyists might be, but the frame alone was worth a fair amount. However, it was an eye catcher, and raised the tone of the whole stall. I wouldn't be disappointed, if it did not sell.

'Penny . . . how's it going?'

I glanced up. Pete stood studying the

paintings, his thumbs stuck in the belt of his tight blue denims. He looked at me and grinned. 'Makin' any money?'

'Not bad.' I was wary, but he was back to his usual cheerful self, as though the previous evening had never been. If he could ignore it, then so could I. 'Pretty well,' I conceded, 'considering the stall was knocked down last night.'

His eyebrows raised. 'It was very windy. Your relatives didn't do such a wonderful job of fixing it up then?'

'Or somebody made a better job of knocking it down,' I retorted.

He frowned, considering what I'd said. 'If it wasn't the wind, then it was one of the Laceys,' he said bluntly, at last.

'Why d'you say that?'

He shrugged. 'Simple enough. Who else had any reason to sabotage things?'

Well — you did for a start, I thought, remembering the fury on his handsome face the last time I'd seen him. I couldn't resist it. 'How's the nose?' I asked mildly.

He fingered it gingerly. 'Could be better. With a head as hard as yours, you should go in for wrestling.'

He looked so rueful, I had to stop myself from smiling. 'Well, I'm sorry about that,' I said sternly. 'I never meant to hurt you — but you did ask for it.'

'I know — I know.' He looked like a small boy, punished for a minor misdeed. Then he grinned, and didn't look penitent at all. 'But you can't blame me for trying!'

I thought it best to change the subject, and bury the hatchet at the same time. 'I've done what you suggested,' I told him, looking properly grateful, ' — about selling some of the smaller paintings in batches. They're going really well. I do think it's going to be a success.'

I was so pleased with myself that I could afford to be nice to Pete, in spite of everything. Then I remembered my earlier suspicions, and fell silent.

He didn't seem to notice, but walked up and down in front of the pictures, assessing them critically. At last he nodded.

'Don't know much about art myself, but you've put them out pretty well, for a beginner. And this big one here, it's an eye-catcher — that's for sure.'

I was pleased to have my judgment reinforced. 'That's what I thought,' I eagerly told him.

''Course,' he said critically, 'you can't sell for toffee apples. Now, if I was doin' it, you wouldn't have a picture left by now.'

'I think I'm doing well enough,' I said stoutly. 'And I'd do even better if people didn't come around taking up my time by chatting to me!'

More people came then, two couples with five small children between them, and I had to keep an eye on things. Small fingers tend to be sticky, and find their way into places they should not be. Still, in spite of that, I managed to sell a bright clown picture for a kiddy's room. It seemed to me that I didn't need to harangue a crowd in order to make sales. People, on the whole, knew what they wanted, and if they saw it — and could afford it — then they would buy. If they didn't like the goods, then nothing would induce them to part with their money. When they'd gone I looked for Pete, but he had disappeared — back to the long-suffering Bert, no doubt.

I was starting to feel quite confident, and it went on like that until lunch-time. Lunch — that was something I hadn't really thought about earlier, but the idea was starting to cause vague stirrings now. I didn't know which was bothering me the more, my poor aching feet, or the insistent murmurings of an empty stomach. I made a firm resolve that the next day I'd bring a stool to sit on, and a flask and some sandwiches. From farther down the row of stalls the smell of hot dogs wafted. Remembering the onions in the one Pete had bought me the day before, my mouth watered. I was really glad of something to take my mind off my growing hunger, when I saw Margaret making her way towards me, with Brian in tow.

'What — you two here again? Can't keep away, is that it?' I joked.

Margaret smoothed down her immaculately-pleated dark blue skirt. 'We thought we should give you some support,' she said defensively. She'd never had much of a sense of humour.

'But shouldn't you be at the Pottery?' I asked Brian.

'No use being a boss, if you can't take time off now and again.' He grinned amiably. 'Anyway, I had business here.'

Business at the market? Then I realised what he meant. The race course edged the land the market used, and today the horses were running — I had been vaguely aware of the noise of the racing crowd, but it had blended into the more immediate noise of the market and so had not registered with me. Pete had hinted that Brian might be overly fond of the sport of kings — I wondered if he was right.

'Anyway,' Brian continued, 'how are you doing . . . finding it tough?'

'Not at all,' I said airily. 'I've had pretty good trade this morning. I reckon everything is going very well.' Then I added, 'The only thing is, I didn't remember to bring any food.'

Margaret clapped her hand to her mouth. 'Oh, Penny, I'm sorry. I should have told you. You must be starving.'

'I'm rather more than that,' I admitted ruefully. 'I'd give anything to have a clean up and sit down for a moment.' I wondered if that sounded too weak-kneed, so I added firmly, 'but I'll get used to it, and it's been fun really.'

Margaret turned to her brother. 'Brian — you could watch the stall for a little while, couldn't you — while I take Penny off for a break?'

'Of course,' he said genially, without a second's hesitation. 'As long as you're back by — ' he glanced at his watch, 'two-thirty.'

'Heavens, we won't be that long.' I laughed. I guessed that two-thirty was most likely the time of the next race. 'I only need time to grab a pastie, or something. Brian — you are a darling.'

I rose on tiptoe and gave him a peck on the cheek. Margaret tugged at my arm. 'Come on, Penny. I want better than a pastie, even if you don't. There's a small cafe by the entrance. We'll go there.'

I unstrapped my money belt and gave it to Brian, and then left arm in arm with Margaret. She was unusually vivacious, turning it into quite an occasion. Poor girl, I thought to myself, I don't suppose she gets many treats these days.

The cafe was packed, no doubt with marketgoers — and possibly racegoers — determined to make a good day of it. We had to wait for a table.

'Grab one when you can,' Margaret said. 'I just must tidy up.'

As she disappeared, straight backed and elegant as ever, I felt amused. Margaret's hair and face were perfection, as usual. I was the one whose hair was beginning to fly around, whose hands felt sticky, and who very decidedly needed to visit the ladies' room! Still — Margaret had always been the fussy one. I waited, and was able to secure us a table by the time she came back.

'My turn now,' I told her with relief. 'You can organise the food. I'll have plaice, chips and peas.' With some difficulty I managed to press money into her unwilling hand. Then I scooted off to the ladies. Eventually, feeling more refreshed, I joined her.

'I hope this will be all right for you' she said uncertainly, peering at the fish. 'They didn't have plaice — only cod.'

I flopped into the chair beside her. 'You're an angel, Margaret. It'll be fine. Just to sit down is marvellous.'

She giggled. 'I know,' she said confidentially. 'The first day I worked the market my ankles swelled up like balloons.'

It was quite fun to sit and have a girlish gossip with her. But something was bothering me, and I had the feeling that Margaret might be able to help.

'Margaret, is it true that Brian is in some kind of financial difficulty?'

She stopped eating, startled, fork halfway to her mouth. 'Who told you that?'

'Oh — just a little bird.'

'Hah!' Her eyes narrowed. 'And I bet the little bird's name was Pete Barlow.'

I just took a sip of coffee, and looked at her over the rim of the cup. 'What is it with the Laceys and Pete Barlow?' I asked at last. 'Pete's hackles rise whenever he sees one of you. Max nearly exploded when he heard I was going out with Pete last night, and you look ready to wring his neck right now!'

She fiddled with her teaspoon. 'I suppose you might as well know. It was my fault, really. Howard had been dead six months, and I — well — I suppose I was vulnerable, and Pete is very persuasive.'

'*You!*' My jaw had dropped. Seeing the amused glances of diners at the other tables, I leaned forward and lowered my voice. 'Margaret, are you telling me there was something between you and Pete Barlow?'

She blushed. Her fair skin had always flamed when she was embarrassed. 'Not — not anything — well, nothing really *happened*.'

'Why not?' I asked with interest. It occurred to me that perhaps a torrid love affair was just what Margaret needed.

She seemed to squirm in her seat. 'Max rescued me in the nick of time — '

I had to laugh. 'Oh, I'm sorry, Margaret — but Max does seem to have a knack of doing that. Were you annoyed — or relieved?'

Her eyes flashed. 'You may take it as a joke, Penny, but I'm not in the habit of behaving that way. It was quite out of character for me, and Max knew it. I was grateful to him, when I came to my senses. Pete just got out of hand, and I realised later that he was only after me because he thought — well, he thought that being a Lacey — '

'You had plenty of money?'

She nodded, and I became thoughtful. Was that why Pete Barlow had taken me out last night? Now that he'd found out I was a better bet than Margaret, had he moved in with an eye to the main chance? After foolishly telling him about the inheritance he might have thought me too good an opportunity to miss. Probably, too, he thought I *was* in the habit of 'behaving that way.' No wonder he was so angry, when foiled a second time. And no wonder Max was angry with me when he found I was going to dinner with Pete.

Well — we learn a little every day. But I still had not found out about Brian.

'But *is* it true, Margaret? About Brian, I mean. Is he in difficulties?'

She had finished her meal, and pushed her plate away. 'I don't really know,' she protested with distaste, giving an ineffectual little wave of her hands. 'He doesn't tell me much. It isn't my business.'

Her look said it wasn't mine either. Perhaps she was right. All the same, her very attitude hinted that what I had heard was true.

It was only half past one, and Margaret decided to go straight back home. She and Brian had come in separate cars, and he would not want to return until later. Plenty of time for Brian to get back to his racing, if that *was* what he was really there for. Entirely his own affair, I told myself. So I said goodbye to Margaret, and hurried back to relieve Brian, feeling refreshed and ready for my afternoon stint.

'There you are,' he greeted me blithely. 'Where's Margaret?'

'She decided to go home.' I stood and checked my stock, turning slowly.

'Have you sold anything?'

He beamed. 'A couple of little things, but guess what . . . I've got rid of your big one.'

'Flatford Mill? You haven't!' But of course he had. I should have noticed immediately that something was missing, right there in the centre on the back wall of the stall. I could have jumped over the moon. Two hundred pounds in one go — on top of what I had already taken. How was that for my first day's trading? What would Max say to that?'

'Aren't you wonderful?' I cried. 'My word, Brian, you Laceys obviously know how to sell. However did you manage it?'

He bloomed under my praise, but tried to look blase about it. 'It was pretty easy. Of course, it was a terrific bargain. I think you'd priced it far too low.'

'Oh, I don't know,' I answered. 'I think it was just about right, really. Come on, Brian, hand over the filthy lucre — I can't wait to count my money!'

He gave me back my money pouch and I eagerly drew out the notes, anticipating a thick wad. But there didn't seem much more than when I had given it to him.'

I held out my hand. 'So — where is it then?'

He looked puzzled. 'It's all there, Penny. There was one small sailing ship picture, one town scene, and twenty pounds for the big one.'

'Twenty pounds!' I stared at him in horror. A cold shiver fingered its way down my spine. I couldn't believe my ears. 'You didn't,' I breathed. 'Oh, Brian, say you didn't sell Flatford Mill for twenty pounds.'

'But of course — ' he faltered, and looked back at me, consternation dawning on his broad face. 'Wasn't that — wasn't it right?'

I tried to pull myself together. Most of the profit I had made during the day had been swallowed in one go. My high spirits drained away.'

'No, I'm afraid it wasn't right, Brian,' I said quietly. 'It should have been *two hundred pounds*.'

'But — but — ' He swung round and pointed to the blackboard. 'Look, it says there — twenty pounds. Doesn't it?'

It did. Somehow the final nought of the price had been erased. Examining it closer I could see the remains of the smudged chalk, where somebody had taken a finger to it.

'How could it have happened?' Brian asked.

I started to speak, gulped and clearing my throat began again, a little steadier this time. 'There were children around earlier on. They must have done it. Don't worry, Brian. It wasn't your fault.'

'I should have known,' he said angrily. 'I was a fool. Trouble is, I don't know much about paintings. If it had been Margaret — or Max even — they'd have known in a tick. I just assumed it was the bargain of the day. I'm so sorry, Penny. I'm afraid this kind of thing happens a lot in the market. And shoplifting — you can lose half your profit that way. But I was in charge . . . I must reimburse you.'

I shook my head angrily. Suspecting what I did about his financial situation, how could I ask him to do that? 'Certainly not — it was no way your fault. I should have checked before I left. I'll have to be more careful, won't I?'

Eventually, with a hangdog expression, he left me, and I carried on trading throughout the afternoon, and made a couple more sales, but the joy had gone out of it for me. I was sure the children had not rubbed out that final nought. I had been watching them like a hawk.

Who else could it have been? Certainly Brian had seemed terribly distressed, and he had offered to make up the difference. If it had been him, he must be a very good actor. But of

144

course, he might have banked on the fact that I would almost certainly refuse his offer. A thought struck me. I only had his word for it that he sold the painting for £20. If he was short of money for the horses, could he have taken the full amount and pocketed the rest?

Then I remembered Pete. He had been hanging around when I was serving the families with the children. I'd been so busy wrapping up the paintings and keeping an eye on the kids, I might not have noticed if he had tampered with the blackboard. And his motive? Well, obviously to get even with me for last night — or a more long-seated grudge against the Lacey family as a whole?

I went through the rest of the day like an automaton, glad when it was over. I felt tired and deflated, having worked all day for practically nothing, but my mind was running in circles like a rat in a trap. How could I find out which of them it had been?

Another thing. Was the person who altered the price on the painting the same one who had slashed the ropes on my stall and tipped it over, in the night?

When the day was over I wearily packed away my remaining stock, checked that all was well with the stall, and wandered through the emptying market towards the linen stall. Pete was round the back, loading great baskets of stuff into their van, so I had a quiet word with Bert.

After I'd made some noncommital remarks about how my first day had gone, I wondered how to broach the subject with him, but I needn't have bothered, because he came up with something that made things clear.

'Cor — what did you do to Lover Boy last night, eh? Gave him a right corker on his conk. Wouldn't stop bleeding. Had to plug it with cotton-wool I did. Up most of the flamin' night.'

'So — so Pete didn't go out again?' I asked tentatively. 'I mean, I thought he might have gone back to the night club.'

Bert snorted. 'Not him! When we finally uncorked him he snored all night. Mind you — did him good, I'll say that. He should know a lady when he sees one.'

I accepted the compliment with a smile, and went on my way with plenty to think about. So it was not Pete who had nearly destroyed my stall. But of course, that didn't altogether clear him of today's little fiasco.

At least this time I need not suspect Max, because he had been nowhere near all day. My spirits lifted at this thought. That was one less person to mistrust. It could have been a complete stranger, people were always milling around. Or it could have been Pete or Brian — but which?

When I returned to Lacey Manor Max had still not come home, and seeing I was in a bad mood, Mrs MacDonald clucked over me and insisted I have a nice long soak before eating. First, however, I felt I must talk to somebody, so I rang Margaret.

I told her what had happened, and she was full of sympathy. 'Oh, that blithering idiot, Brian,' she fumed. 'Such a fool. His own commonsense should have told him the painting was worth more than twenty pounds. I'd have known.'

'That's just what Brian said,' I told her with a shaky laugh. 'He said you or Max would have known, but you had gone home, and of course Max was nowhere around.'

'Oh, but he was!' Her voice was blithely unconcerned over the phone. 'Didn't you know? He popped round to see how you were getting on, while we were at lunch. Apparently he had a chat with Brian, and then pushed off again. I gave him a ring at work, because he'd asked me to keep an eye on you, but he said he'd seen for himself how well you were doing. She'll make her fortune, he told me.'

'Did he now?' I murmured, and felt sick. 'Did he indeed?'

7

I lay back in the ivory-coloured bath, and moodily looked at my toes as they poked through the bubbles. It was a sumptuous bathroom, every girl's dream; not quite in the gold-plated taps bracket, but not far off. Any other time I would have wallowed in the unaccustomed luxury, but this time my mind was otherwise occupied.

So Max was back in the running as a suspect? The idea lay sourly on my mind, the perfect end to a perfect day! Suddenly I was sick to death of the whole thing. What had started out as an exciting adventure had now become something drab and sullied by suspicion. I liked all of my relatives — in varying amounts. How could I think that one of them was out to deliberately sabotage me? With a heavy sigh I pulled out the plug, and stepped out of the bath on to the thick bath mat. As I towelled myself, my mind was going in circles.

What else could I think? Too much had happened since the day of the funeral — and much of it unpleasant. First, there was the way my goods had been thrown on the courtyard floor, the night I arrived. There had been something definitely nasty about that — not just the deliberate viciousness of it, but the calculated contempt, as though my paintings were utter rubbish. Who could have been responsible for that, the first of the attacks? Any of the Laceys, I decided — but not Pete, because he had not known of my existence at that time.

Then there was the near destruction of my stall in the middle of the night. Again, it could have been anybody — except Pete, according to Bert — and I believed him. If Pete had gone out again that night, Bert would surely have known.

Finally, there was the erasure of the

final nought from the price of the Flatford Mill painting. That was the most serious to date. The other incidents had been annoying, but this had cost me a lot of money. And this time the culprit could have been anyone — the Laceys, Pete, or even a member of the public.

Thoughtfully I slipped into my bathrobe and slippers, and padded my way back to my bedroom, my mind following the same train of thought. In a dream I put on a comfortable yellow track suit, and an old pair of trainers, and sat on the bed, trying to brush some semblance of order into my wiry mop of hair. Moodily I regarded my reflection in the dressing table mirror. I was wearing what my mother called my 'thundercloud' look. Dark eyes looked back at me, resentfully. Full lips were compressed in an indignant line. What joy had this inheritance brought me so far? None at all, that I could see. I hadn't sought it — and now I was even less sure that I wanted it at all. Did I even *care* who it was that was out to destroy me?

Was I afraid to know the answer?

Abruptly I flung the brush down. Of course I had to know. However much it hurt — even if it destroyed the dreams I'd clung to over the years. I had to know.

So, I had to be sensible. And the first thing I must consider was — motive.

If I'd still been able to count Pete amongst the suspects it would have been easy. Plain jealousy — of the Laceys in general, and of my treatment of him in particular. That would have been obvious enough. But it looked more and more as though I must cross Pete off my list. And that left —

Margaret or Brian?

The same motive could apply to both, of course. Margaret probably felt that Great-aunt Penelope should have left more money to her — as she had children to support. But Margaret had been nothing but friendly to me, and I *had* told her I would pay for the boys' education. I remembered, that had been before the last two incidents — and so it seemed highly unlikely that it could be her. I smiled at the thought. In any case, I could hardly imagine the fluttery and fastidious Margaret doing such things. Which brought me to Brian.

Brian? Well — that was another kettle of fish. Brian had been nice, too — but if he was a gambler, and if his firm was in financial difficulties — that put quite a different complexion on things. I didn't like to think it of him. It argued a side to his character that I had never known — but Mrs MacDonald had warned me, hadn't she?

Finally — there was Max. What could his motive be? Did he need the money? It didn't seem so — but how could I tell? He might have debts I knew nothing about. The business might be in difficulties. And he *was* the head of the Laceys now. With his strong sense of family pride, perhaps he felt it wrong that I should have Great-aunt

Penelope's wealth. Besides which, I thought miserably, he disapproved of me so much. He always had — ever since that night.

'Blast you, Great-aunt Penelope. And blast your inheritance, too!'

I stormed out of the bedroom and down the wide staircase. Mrs MacDonald had lit a fire in the sitting-room, and I curled up in one of the big squashy armchairs. Perhaps I should forget the whole thing. Perhaps it would be better to quit now, and ask for my old job back. I was sure I could get it. Better to leave all this suspicion and nastiness behind, and live an ordinary life.

But as soon as that thought came to me I realised it was precisely what somebody was trying to make me feel. I felt my cheeks burn with anger and my chin went up stubbornly. Well — I wasn't about to give anyone the satisfaction of making me turn tail. I would work my year at the stall, and *when* I had done so successfully, and *when* I had received the inheritance, then I would turn and throw it all in their faces and tell them what they could do with it. Even Max. Oh, Max!

Mrs MacDonald came in then to tell me that she was going home, and to ask whether I wanted anything. 'No,' I told her miserably. 'I don't want anything.' She gave me a dark look, and a sigh, and went off shaking her head.

I gazed into the flames for some time, and then buried my face in one of the cushions and gave way to the unhappiness I was feeling. Why hadn't I stayed away? I was in love with Max. I always had been — I always would be. It didn't even seem to make any difference that he might be the one who was working against me.

'Penny!'

I jumped to my feet. I hadn't heard him come in, and I stood foolishly staring at him, the tears still wet on my cheeks.

'My sweet girl!'

I don't know if he stepped towards

me, or if I flung myself at him, but somehow I was in his arms, and he was stroking my hair. He was wiping my tears, murmuring things, wonderful, crazy, unlikely things. I couldn't believe my ears and I turned my face up to his in bewilderment. He shook his head helplessly. 'Don't cry. Penny, my poor darling — don't cry — I can't bear it!'

His lips found mine, and I was whirling in a maelstrom of sweet sensation, hardly able to think. I just clung to him, half laughing, half crying, kissing him back with every ounce of my strength. I couldn't understand it, and I didn't care. I only lived in this one moment, afraid it might burst like a bubble, leaving me as miserable as I had been before.

My knees felt weak, which was perhaps how we came to almost collapse on to the settee. He cradled me in his arms, almost crooning. 'My poor love. You mustn't upset yourself. It was only one picture — you'll make it up.'

So that was what he was on

about — he thought I was crying about that. I could have laughed. It didn't matter a jot — not now. But I didn't care about the reason — until a horrid little worm of unease wriggled through my mind. 'How — how did you know about the picture?' I breathed.

'Brian told me,' he said easily. 'We had dinner out together tonight — we had some business to discuss. Otherwise, I'd have returned sooner, once I knew. I guessed you'd be upset. It was a rotten thing to happen on your first day.'

Relief poured through me. 'I'm all right. Really, Max. It just — well it just suddenly got a bit too much for me.'

'You really are still a kid at heart, aren't you?' he murmured. 'In spite of that hard facade, you're as soft as they come.'

'Hard? Me!' I was shocked. Was that how I appeared to him. 'I didn't know I gave that impression,' I said slowly. 'No wonder you disliked me so.'

'Disliked you?' He cupped my chin in

his hand and tuned my face up to his, smiling down at me with those dark grey eyes. 'What gave you that funny idea?'

'Well — ' I didn't want to drag up the many times we seemed to have drawn sparks from one another. Not now. 'You certainly gave that impression that time — you know — when I was here before.'

He chuckled. 'Oh — that.'

'Yes, that!' I retorted, indignant about past hurts. 'You didn't have to be so cruel. Why did you fetch Great-aunt Penelope to the bedroom? I needed you then, Max. I wanted to stay here, and Mother was planning on taking me away. If you wanted to throw me out, you could at least have done it yourself.'

He kissed me gently on each corner of my mouth. 'Did it never occur to you, sweet girl, that I was afraid to deal with it myself. That I couldn't trust myself!'

I shook my head, bemused both by his kisses and by what he was suggesting. 'I don't understand.'

'Oh, Penny!' His face creased with sudden amusement. 'You should have seen yourself as I saw you! You were so young, and I had fallen for you hook, line and sinker. I knew you had a schoolgirl crush on me. That was all it was. I knew it, and I knew I mustn't take advantage of it. That was why I had to keep my distance. That was why I didn't dare touch you. Don't you see . . . ?'

My eyes searched his face. He nodded. 'I wanted you then. Perhaps I'd built up a strong façade, too, to protect myself. To protect us both. I almost came to believe in it myself. When you turned up again I found I still wanted you. It made me feel — unsure of myself. I tried to fight it. Told myself it was nothing but physical attraction — but when I saw you in tears tonight I knew it was more. I love you, Penny.'

I rubbed my head against his shoulder. 'Do you still think I have a

159

schoolgirl crush?'

He said no more, but his arms tightened around me and his kisses were warm and tender. My arms curled around his neck. It was true. He had told me so. He loved me.

We stayed there until late into the night, talking silly inconsequential things that mattered to no-one but ourselves. It wasn't until the wood fire burned down to powdery white ash, and I began to yawn in spite of myself, that I realised how tired I was.

'Poor love.' He nuzzled his face into my hair and kissed my ear. 'You're dead beat. It's bed for you.' He scooped me up and carried me up the stairs like a baby. When we stopped outside my bedroom door I half expected him to take me inside. I half *wanted* him to, and yet part of me wasn't ready yet. But instead he just held me close, and kissed me again. 'Sleep well, Pennywise.'

I tumbled into bed, hugging the memory of his kisses to me. Warm and content, I expected to fall asleep straight away, but instead I found myself wide awake. It was so hard to believe — so wonderful, but so unbelievable, that Max should have been in love with me all those years ago. That he should love me still. After all, I'd been a mere child then, and he had been an eligible young man. Why me?

I tried to thrust these thoughts from me, but they continued to niggle. The wonderful, safe, warm feeling began to drain away. I wanted to believe — oh, how much I wanted to . . .

In the end I couldn't lie in bed any longer. I got up, and put on my dressing gown. I paced the bedroom, thinking and wondering until my head felt heavy and hot. To cool it I went across to the window and pulled back the curtains, leaning my forehead against the glass. It was bright moonlight outside. I could see the courtyard, the barn I was using as a studio.

Idly I noticed that the studio door was open, and I cursed. That had been careless of me. I thought I'd locked it and left the key on the top ledge of the door — where we always left keys at Lacey Court, so that any other member of the family could enter if they wanted to. It had been a reflex action. Well — I must have been mistaken. Now I'd have to go down and lock it, or I wouldn't have a moment's peace.

Quietly, I left my room, and went down the stairs, the round window above the stairs letting in enough light for me to see by. I went through the kitchen, unlocking its door and letting myself out. I shivered and drew my dressing gown closer around me; it was cold out. Hurrying, I crossed the courtyard to the barn, and as I grew near I realised that I could see a glow through the open doorway. My heart skipped a beat. 'No!' I shouted. 'Oh — no!'

Running I reached the door and flung it wider open. The barn was lit up inside, glowing from the fire that was burning at the far end of my studio — a fire fed by some of my paintings, and a great heap of my frames. The flames were reaching higher, smoke filling the interior, the heat already enough to scorch my face. Soon the whole place would go up in smoke.

It was too much for me to handle. I backed out, slamming the door shut. Then I turned and faced the house. Looking up at the bedroom windows. 'Max!' I shrieked. I cupped my hands to my mouth. 'Max. Max, help!'

For a moment there was no reply, and I dithered, not knowing what to do next. Then his window opened, and could sense him there, rather than see him. 'The barn's on fire!' I yelled. 'Max, help me!'

I didn't wait to see what he would do. There was a rake leaning against the barn wall, and I snatched it up. Opening the door again, I plunged in. Coughing and spluttering I tried to rake away some of the wooden frames, in the hope that if the fire was starved of anything inflammable it might burn itself out. The stone walls of the barn would not ignite — but of course the roof timbers could catch. Thank goodness the roof was of tiles, and not thatch. A spark landed on the hem of my dressing gown, and I had to drop the rake to beat at it.

'Penny — for goodness' sake, get out of here.'

Max spun me round by my shoulders, and pushed me into the open air, where I bent over, coughing and spluttering. Then he picked up something he'd been carrying, and I saw it was the fire extinguisher that was always kept in a corner of the kitchen near the door. He disappeared into the barn, and I sagged against the wall, holding my face in my hands.

'Max — be careful,' I croaked.

It seemed an age, while I listened in dread to the crackling become a hissing. Then all went quiet.

'Max . . . ?' I stepped slowly towards the barn door, afraid of what I might see. Then he appeared in the doorway.

I flung myself forward, my arms reaching for him. 'Oh . . . I was so afraid you'd get hurt. You *are* all right, aren't you?' I held him away from me. 'You're not burnt?'

'I'm fine. I was scared for you.' He hugged me fiercely. 'You shouldn't have gone in there, you little goose,' he scolded.

For once I didn't snap back. 'Is it bad?' I asked quietly.

'I'm not sure. Shall we see? I want to check that it's properly out.

Strangely enough the fire had not damaged the electric wiring in the barn, and we were able to switch on the lights. A very sorry sight met our eyes. There was a layer of black on every surface, and the heap in the far corner was nothing more than a charred and blackened mess. I got the rake, and poked it tentatively.

'From what I can see, it was only the loose canvases that were on the fire. Look, I still have a carton full over here. And I have more, up in that loft section. It's the frames that have suffered mostly.'

Max looked angry and determined. 'I suppose it isn't much use my asking if it could have been an accident.'

'No,' I said bluntly. 'It isn't. If you suggested it was, I wouldn't believe you. This was quite deliberate. If I hadn't seen it the whole place might have gone up. It's a good thing the house is on the opposite side of the courtyard, or that might have caught.'

'As it was,' he said quietly, 'you could have been hurt — even killed.' He clutched me to him again, so tightly that it hurt. 'This has gone far enough,' he muttered. 'It's got to stop. Penny, promise you'll marry me. Promise me now.' He kissed my lips, my face, my eyes. 'You do love me, don't you?'

'Oh, Max!' I was in a spinning haze of delight. As if that needed to be asked. Of course I would marry him. It was all in the world that I ever wanted to do. All I had ever dreamed about. Then he was talking again.

'Look at you, you're nearly out on your feet. Marry me, and give up all this market nonsense, Penny. Marry me and forget about it.'

I felt a cold shudder run down my spine. Gently I disengaged myself from his arms. His face was in shadow. 'Max, I'm worn out, as you've just said,' I pleaded. 'Please . . . can we talk about it tomorrow?'

'Of course!'

He quickly made one more inspection to make sure that there were no lingering sparks, and then we made our way back to the house, his arm around my waist. I felt chilled to the very bone, but it was not because of the night air.

'Are you sure you're all right?' Max asked me when we were inside. 'Let me get you a brandy.'

'No, really.' I smiled wanly. 'One way or another, it's been quite a day. All I need is a peaceful night's sleep. Goodnight, Max. See you in the morning.'

He kissed me again, and I did not

respond with quite the same fervour, he must have put it down to tiredness, for he let me go and I climbed the stairs to my bedroom. Once there I washed the grime off me, and crawled into my bed, my head aching. My mind was a jumble of thoughts and feelings.

Max wanted me to give up the market stall. That was the over-riding thought that kept tearing at me. He could have engineered the fire, hoping it would be the final straw that would make me give in.

I lay staring into the darkness. It couldn't have been Max . . . could it? I couldn't believe it of him. But then, could I trust my own judgment? One thing was certain, I couldn't go on like this, not knowing. If Max felt driven to such lengths, how much further would he go? And there was no need, that was the silly part of it. If he married me the money would be as good as his.

Then another horrible thought struck me. Perhaps all his talk of love had been made up on the spur of the moment

— just a safeguard, in case I couldn't be frightened off. He wouldn't really want to saddle himself with a wife he didn't love.

Ah, yes! That was the most hurtful thing of all. He would have strung me along until I gave up the whole idea of the market — and then what would have happened? Would he have found we were not suited, perhaps?

I tossed and turned. But supposing I was wrong? Suppose it was not Max who was to blame, but Brian?

It seemed to be nearly morning, before I came to any conclusion. Then I knew what I had to do.

8

The next morning, as soon as I'd dressed, I went downstairs and picked up the telephone in the hall. I knew that, with two lively boys to look after, Margaret would not be lying in bed late, and sure enough she answered the phone instantly.

'Margaret — I'm sorry to get you up so early, but I have a favour to ask.'

'Of course, Penny. Anything I can do?'

I glanced up the stairs. There was no sign of Max yet. I kept my lips close to the mouthpiece of the phone. 'Yes, as a matter of fact, there is. I can't explain now, but could you make some excuse for getting Brian to come to the market today? I'll explain later.'

'Well, yes, I suppose so.'

She didn't ask me why, and I was glad, because I felt too tired, and too uncertain of what I was doing, to go into long explanations at that moment. I had a plan. It might be badly thought out. It might be crazy. But if it worked, I would know, once and for all, the answers to all my questions. And then? Well, that would depend on what I discovered. I replaced the phone softly, and stood thinking.

'Darling! Here you are, Penny-wise.'

Max came up behind me, cradling me in his arms, nuzzling into my hair. I leaned against him with a sigh, and closed my eyes. What heaven this would be, if only . . .

'Who were you ringing?'

'Oh, only Margaret,' I told him truthfully, and then — with a horrible feeling that I was doing the wrong thing, prepared to lie. 'She told me yesterday that she might see me in the market today. I was just ringing to see if she'd changed her mind.'

He turned me around, and held me away from him. His dark grey eyes were looking anxious. He touched my cheek gently. 'You're surely not going in today?'

My smile was bright. 'But of course, Max. Why ever shouldn't I?'

'But.' He stopped, and looked non-plussed, as if he had been going to say something, and had changed his mind. 'Are you sure you'll have enough stock to sell, after the fire?'

I nodded. 'Oh, yes. I had quite a lot still in the van, and with what I'd stacked away, up in the loft, there's plenty.'

He pulled me to him, and kissed me. It was a very satisfactory kiss, and I tried to put everything else out of my mind, and just enjoy what I had. My arms went around his neck, as he pulled my body close to his. I could feel his breathing quicken, and I was by no means unmoved myself! We seemed to be melted together for an age, and then at last his grasp slackened, and I leaned away.

'Wow!' I said.

He grinned. 'A very descriptive

remark!' Then his grin faded. 'But are you fit to go in today? You had a pretty hard time of it yesterday — and then the fire last night.'

He was persuasive, but I was more stubborn. I placed my fingers over his lips. 'Max, I'm a very tough lady, I'll have you know. Nothing is going to stop me from going in.'

He frowned. 'But you won't have your special exhibition painting — the one that sold for twenty pounds.'

'No,' I agreed. 'I can manage without it this morning. But when I get back this afternoon I'm going to clean out the barn, and then I'll frame another one. I'm collecting it from town today. Actually, it's waiting for me at the post office — I have some duty to pay on it. It's a rather better one than the other. If I manage to sell it, I'll more than recoup my losses. I hope so, at least, because it cost me quite a bit.'

He frowned. 'Well, don't overdo things. Promise me.'

'I promise.' He kissed me again, and I almost faltered in what I'd decided to do. But then I rushed on. 'As a matter of fact, once I've framed that one I'm going to pop back into town. I've managed a late hair appointment.'

'Good,' he said. 'You need a break.' Feeling like a Judas, I raised my face for another kiss, and as his arms tightened around me I told myself that no matter what happened, I loved him. I couldn't imagine that he had ever meant me any harm. Even last night, he had only meant to damage a few of my paintings. It had been sheer bad luck that I had discovered the fire. No doubt, if I had not gone down then, he would have doused the flames before things got out of hand. That is — if it *was* Max. I still hoped it was not. But better to know, to bring it out into the open. Maybe there would be some hope for us then. If he saw how stupid it all was, if he saw that I didn't care.

But, no matter what, we had to clear

this between us. Otherwise, if I just took what he offered and married him, it would always be there, like a ghost at the wedding, and I would always wonder. Max or Brian?

'Max,' I said at last. 'I must go now, or I'll be late.'

He held me tightly for a moment, his cheek against my hair. 'I wish I could come with you, but this morning I have an important meeting.'

'I'll be all right.' I laughed. 'Really. What could possibly go wrong?'

He held me away from him by my shoulders, his eyes scanning my face, and I was shocked to see him looking drawn and haggard.

'I don't know,' he said slowly. 'I wish I did. Penny, let me announce our wedding. Give up the idea of the market.'

'No,' I answered stubbornly.

'I thought you loved me.'

'And I thought *you* loved *me*! Max, too much has been happening, you must give me time.'

His hands dropped to his sides. 'If that's your last word,' he said a little stiffly.

I reached on tiptoe and gave him a little kiss on the corner of his mouth. 'It is. But don't look so glum. I do love you.'

'Oh, Penny . . .'

He swung on his heel, and went out, and a minute later I heard his car drive away, and I wondered — why had his cry held so much love, and so much desperation? I left soon after, on my way to the market.

It was a busy morning, and I did quite a bit of trade. I was beginning to find my feet now, and it didn't seem quite so strange. I would have been enjoying it, if it hadn't been for a horrible sick feeling in my stomach. Had I done right? I wondered. I assured myself that I had. By this evening, I would know the worst. That is . . . if my plan worked . . .

Pete visited me. 'How's it going?'

'Not bad,' I told him. 'Did you hear

about the fire at Lacey Court last night?'

His eyebrows raised. 'No — bad?'

I shrugged. 'Only my studio. Some of my paintings burnt.'

He whistled. 'That's bad luck. How did it happen?'

'We don't know,' I said with a dead-pan expression. 'I must have dropped a spark on to something dry — I *had* been heating up some varnish.'

'Did you lose much?' he asked.

'A fair bit. But I can soon replace them. I've got a really valuable one to sell. I'm going to frame it this afternoon. You'll probably see it here tomorrow.'

After a short conversation he left me to return to his own stall. Two down, I thought grimly, and one to go.

I'd made sure this time that I'd brought a stool, a Thermos of hot coffee, and some sandwiches, and so I was able to have lunch on the spot, with only a quick sortie to the ladies while the man on the stall next to mine kept an eye on things. It was well into the afternoon before Margaret turned up with Brian.

'Here we are again,' he greeted me with a cheerful grin. 'Can't seem to keep away, can we? Can't blame me this time, my dear sister here dragged me along — goodness knows why.'

'I told you — the boys have been invited to friends, and so I wanted to get out — to have lunch. Anyway, I wanted a chat with Penny, and I didn't feel like driving myself.'

She leaned forward and gave me a kiss on my cheek. Her lips felt cool, and she wafted a light perfume. She had done her part — now it was up to me.

'I'm glad to see you both,' I said gloomily. 'Did Max tell you what happened last night?'

Brian shook his head. 'Last night?' Margaret echoed. 'You mean, after you phoned?'

I nodded. 'Quite a while later. Some paintings in my barn caught on fire, half my stock went up in flames.'

'Oh no!' Margaret's hand went to her mouth. 'How awful for you, Penny. You weren't hurt?'

'You can see she wasn't,' Brian said gruffly. 'Look, Pen, I feel even worse now. About yesterday, I mean. Losing such a lot on that sale, and then losing more of your pictures.'

I smiled wanly. 'Not the best of starts, is it?'

Then I straightened up. 'Still — I've got a chance to recoup some of my losses. I'm going to frame some more when I get back today. I've got one beauty. That alone will make up for everything.' Then I pulled a face. 'If it wasn't for that . . . well, I do believe I'd give up altogether. Perhaps I'm not cut out for this kind of thing. After all, money isn't everything.'

'I wish I could do more to help,' Brian said. 'But I expect Max will be of more use.'

I smiled at him. 'I'd rather work alone, thank you. It won't take me long. Then Max and I are going out to drown my sorrows!'

We weren't, but Brian was not to know that. I wanted him to think the coast would be clear for him to have another go . . . if it was him. How I hated all this uncertainty.

We chatted for a little while longer, and Brian offered to let me go to lunch with Margaret again, but I declined. 'I've got my sandwiches and a Thermos,' I told him.

'I'll stay with you for a while,' Margaret said loyally. 'Go and get lost for a while, Brian. I want to chat to Penny — girl's talk.'

I offered her the stool, but she just leaned against the corner of the stall, her head cocked on one side. When Brian moved away, she accused me. 'What are you playing at? You aren't really meaning to give up, are you?'

I smiled ruefully. 'Am I such a bad actor?'

She shook her head. 'No, but I know you. You never were a quitter, and I feel sure you're not now. So, what is all this about?'

How was I to tell her? Whichever way I put it I was accusing one of her brothers of deliberately trying to rob me of my inheritance. But there was no way out of it. I had better just come clean.

'You're right,' I said. 'The trouble is, *somebody* is trying to sabotage my business. And I don't know who. It boils down to three, well, two really, because it began before I even met Pete. So, I'm afraid that only leaves — '

'Brian or Max?'

I nodded unhappily.

'Or me,' she suggested with a little smile. Then she frowned. 'I can't say I like this, Penny. Blood is thicker than water. What will you do when you find out, the police . . . ?'

'Oh, no!' I said, shocked. 'Nothing like that. It's just, well, you see, I just *have* to know.'

'So what are you planning to do.'

'I'm going to do what I said I was

181

going to do, my framing. But I'm not going to leave it at that. Brian will reckon I've gone out with Max, and Max'll think I've gone to the hairdressers — I'll hide the van round the back. When whoever it is comes to the barn . . . well, then I'll be lying in wait.'

She chewed her lip. 'Penny,' she said at last. 'Can't you see what this will do to the family? Wouldn't it — well, wouldn't it be better if you just gave up and went away? You'd get your fair share of the money. Max would see to that, you could be sure. Wouldn't it be fairer, and less painful, all round?'

She was right. If I hadn't been in love with Max, I would have agreed whole heartedly, but I had no choice. I couldn't go through life always wondering — wondering.

Did Max *really* love me? If I married him, never knowing the truth, what kind of a life would that be, with this always hanging between us. Whether he was guilty, or innocent — the result would be the same. The only other thing I could do would be to leave him. To throw away his love, and go back to London, my tail between my legs, and forget Max Lacey for ever.

And that I was not prepared to do.

I shook my head. 'I can't, Margaret. Things have gone too far now. I can't give up.'

She sighed, and I noticed her complexion was paler than ever. All this was obviously distressing her, and I was sorry to have brought it on her. 'So, nothing I can say will persuade you, I suppose?' she said quietly. 'You are determined to go through with it?'

'Yes, Margaret,' I said steadily, knowing I was taking an irrevocable step. 'I'm going to see this through, to the bitter end.'

And bitter it might well be, I thought sadly as I packed my things up later that day. Margaret had staunchly offered to come and keep watch with me, but I had refused her help. It would be bad enough confronting either Max, or Brian. How much worse would it be

183

for her, for either way it must be one of her brothers who was involved. I could at least spare her the embarrassment of the ensuing scene.

Having once set my mind to what I had to do, I wasted no time. Back at Lacey Court I had a quick meal, and then went out to the barn. In the harsh light of day, my paintings looked a sorry sight. I raked them out into the yard, and then scooped them up into a rubbish bin. After that I scrubbed out the remaining ashes, and then set about cleaning the greasy smuts off the remainder of my stock. When I reckoned enough time had been spent doing that, I climbed up into the loft and brought down a canvas. In actual fact, I had lied when I said it was expensive — it was only large, but that didn't matter. I framed it, and set it up on an easel. The cheese was in the trap. All I had to do now was to set the spring.

I left the barn, locking the door behind me, and reached up to leave the key in its usual place on the ledge. Then I went back to the house, cleaned myself up, and changed into the fresh jeans, a dark top, and a pair of sneakers. That done, I reckoned that if anyone had been watching they would have had plenty of time to decide what they were going to do. I said goodbye to Mrs MacDonald, telling her I was going out. I got into the van, and drove down the drive. But when I came to the end of it, out of sight of the house and anyone watching, I didn't turn off down the main road, but followed a track that led into the wood.

I parked there, and left the car, following a little path I knew so well, until I doubled back to behind the barn. There was a big old tree growing close by, and one of its branches reached out until it touched the roof of the building, and in that roof was a skylight, leading into the loft.

The tree was an easy one to climb; I had often perched up in its branches when I had last been at Lacey Court, and I had no great difficulty in getting up there now. Once on the roof I ran across the old tiles, crouching so that I would not be seen over the shallow ridge, until I came to the skylight. It was open, because I'd left it that way, on purpose. I slid my hand in, moved the latch, and pulled the glass up. The opening was not very large — but then, I was not all that big either, and after much wriggling, I worked my way through, and landed on the dusty floor of the loft. Now there was nothing left for me to do but wait.

Minute followed minute, each one seeming longer as I lay up there, wondering whether I had succeeded in fooling any watcher . . . and trying to rehearse what I would say when the culprit — IF the culprit — did arrive. It had been one thing to plan this, and it had been exciting carrying out the plan. But to wait in cold blood, was a different matter.

Whoever came through that door, I would give them time to make their intentions quite plain — I wanted no mistakes. I shifted uneasily. The floor was hard, with nothing but an old sack to lie on, but all I would have to do was raise my head. I couldn't see the door from my position, but once an intruder moved forward I would have a clear view of the easel and the canvas — and whoever had been sabotaging me. What was troubling me more than anything was the persistent thought — if it were Max, if it were Max, then what?

What could I say to him? Could I convince him that I cared for him, no matter what, so long as he loved me? Or would I find that, once discovered, his love had been nothing but a hollow sham, and there was nothing left but bitterness and pain? After all — I didn't seem to be a very good judge of men. Simon had proved a broken reed. Pete was after my money. And Max? If only I knew!

I laid my head on my arms, and lay there, wishing none of this was happening, but knowing it must.

After a while I heard a car draw up. Max coming home, perhaps. There was no way of knowing, and so I remained, tense and on edge, and waited some more. Nothing happened. Perhaps I would have to wait all night. At what time should I give in, and admit it had all been a complete waste of time?

I must have been there at least another hour, and getting very cold and stiff, when I heard a movement outside. My heart raced. This was it!

There was another sound — a light footstep. Then a scratching at the door. The key turned in the lock. The door squeaked as it was pushed open — I held my breath — the door closed, and I heard more squeaky sounds. I counted to ten, then raised my head.

'Margaret!'

My yell of disappointment made her jump. She whirled around, and stared up to see me looking down on her. She looked incongruously out of place, so neat and tidy in her cream two-piece, a row of pearls around her neck and a large handbag over her arm. Not at all what I had been hoping — or fearing — would take the bait.

'Oh, so you were up there,' she said calmly. 'I was wondering where you'd be hiding.'

I could have shaken her. There was no likelihood that anyone would come now, with her car parked outside. I scrabbled to my feet, swung myself through the hatch and climbed down the ladder.

'What did you come for, Margaret?' I scolded. 'I *told* you not to. Now you've ruined everything.'

She waited for me, calm as ever. 'Do you really think so?'

'Yes I do!' I shouted, reaction making my temper short. 'I was all ready and waiting. Neither Max or Brian would risk coming here now. You've spoiled it all.'

She shook her head, and began rummaging in her bag. 'Not yet, Penny dear. For a start, I haven't yet spoiled — this!'

189

Her hand came out of the bag, and then shot forward to the canvas. There was the glint of a blade, as she slashed and tore like a wild thing. I couldn't speak. I couldn't move. Not Margaret! Not like this, it wasn't possible.

She was laughing, and sobbing, panting in the fury of her sudden attack, and I simply stood there rooted to the spot in amazement. Her handbag dropped to the floor, unheeded. The painting rocked on the easel, and she grabbed at it with her left hand, as she went on stabbing.

'Margaret — you. It was you all the time!'

She laughed. Her hair was flying loose, untidy for the first time since I'd known her. She turned, and my blood ran cold. Her eyes were glazed and quite crazy, a little blob of spittle at the corner of her mouth.

'That's spoiled now, isn't it. Penny?' she asked — her voice all the more terrifying for its gentle note of inquiry. 'Quite, quite spoiled. You will have lost all your money now. You won't get your inheritance.'

I didn't stop to think. 'That picture wasn't worth hardly anything, Margaret. Just a cheap copy. Surely you would have known?'

She looked uncomprehending at first. Then stared at the remains of the canvas. She gave a shriek of rage. 'You cheated! You said if you lost this you'd give up.'

She advanced towards me, the knife held in front of her. It looked long and vicious — something from the kitchen no doubt — and from the way it had sliced throught the tough canvas, it was sharp, too. I backed away. Keep her talking, that was what I had to do.

'But, Margaret, I don't understand. Was it you, the first night I came?'

She nodded eagerly, but she stopped advancing. 'I thought that would be enough, perhaps. But you always were stubborn, Penny.'

'And the stall — the night of the storm?' I could hardly believe that, but then I remembered that Margaret had been used to lumping around great concrete garden ornaments. She wasn't really the delicate, ineffectual person I had always thought.

She nodded again. 'That shook you, eh?' She frowned. 'Of course, it would have slowed you up more, if it hadn't been for Max. He was a fool. He shouldn't have been helping you. I didn't expect it — not after what had happened before between you. I thought he'd be glad.'

'Max is coming here any minute,' I said hopefully, but it was useless.

'No . . . no,' she said with a note of reproof in her voice. 'Max has gone out. Mrs MacDonald told me. And Brian — ' She smiled. 'Well, Brian won't be coming, will he? Because Brian never had anything to do with it.'

'And of course you were with me at the market, the day the price was changed on Flatford Mill.' I didn't need her to confirm that. It all clicked into place now. The way she had insisted on going to wash her hands at the cafe. There would have been tell-tale chalk on her fingers. Oh, yes, she had been a cool one, all right.

'But, Margaret,' I protested. 'I can understand your not wanting me to succeed at first. But I told you I would help with the boys' education, and . . . '

'Charity!' She spat the word at me, her face contorted, and waved the knife in front of my eyes. 'Charity! D'you think I want to live on your left-overs? The money should have been mine. Mine — and my children's — d'you hear me?'

I took another step backwards. If I could turn her a little I would make a dash for the door. 'But there was Max, and Brian.'

'No.' She almost screamed. 'They'd had their chance. But what chance have I had? Penelope should have left the money to me. But instead, she chose fit to throw it away on a little, a little . . . '

She had been advancing, and I had been retreating, but I had worked around in a small circle, and at last I saw my chance. I flung myself at the door. And tugged. And tugged.

Margaret burst into peals of laughter. 'The key's in my bag, Penny, dear. There's no way you can get out.'

She was smiling at me, maliciously, and I could see that her tenuous grip on reality had snapped. She had always been obsessively attached to someone. Now it was her children — and her mother-love had taken her beyond the bounds of reason. She was quite mad.

I looked hopefully towards the loft, but Margaret was between me and the ladder. Even if I *could* scramble up, it would be useless. There was no way I could struggle through a skylight quickly enough to evade a plunging knife.

'What — what are you going to do?' I asked through lips stiff with fear.

She took another step towards me. 'I've thought it all out,' she said conversationally. 'I'll have to kill you of course. Then I'll put you in the boot of my car, and dispose of you. In the woods. I'll tell Max you decided you'd had enough.' She nodded. 'He'll believe me. He knows we get on well together.' She giggled again. 'It was worth it, fawning over you, when, Penny, *dear*, I could hardly stand being near you. Oh, yes. I have it all worked out.'

It was crazy. Only a mad woman would have imagined that such a plan would succeed. But, then, Margaret *was* mad, so much was distressingly obvious now. It was useless to plead with her, but I found myself pleading all the same.

I held out my hands. 'Margaret — you can't do this. Max will be angry.'

She shook her head. 'No, Penny. Max will be angry with you — for leaving. Yes, he will be *very* angry with you.'

Then suddenly she must have tired of talking, and without any warning, she sprang. I gave a scream and jumped backwards, tripping over something, and going sprawling. I saw her triumphant smile as she raised the knife above me.

Then a heavy body hurtled down from the loft, and Margaret went flying, her mouth a round O of surprise. I heard shouting — Margaret's voice unfamiliar with rage, screaming and cursing. And that was the last I heard, as everything swirled, and I felt myself sinking into merciful blackness.

I opened my eyes to morning sunlight pouring through the window of my bedroom. For a moment I forgot what had happened. I stretched, and yawned. I'd better get up, I thought. Another day at the market — I was quite looking forward to it.

Then remembrance flooded in with an uprush of panic, and I started bolt upright in bed.

'Margaret!'

Mrs MacDonald was sitting on the end of the bed. She pushed me back on to the bed. 'It's all right. You're quite safe. You've got to rest, the doctor says so. You've had a nasty shock.'

I hardly dared ask. 'But Margaret — what happened?'

She looked sad. 'They've taken her away, my dear. But it's the best thing that could happen.'

I raised my hand and rubbed it across my eyes, to clear them. 'You knew all along, didn't you?'

She looked quite indignant. 'No, I never knew!' She shrugged. 'I was just worried. I've known Margaret a long time. She was always highly strung, and since Howard died she's been difficult. There have been — incidents — but there's someone else who can tell you better than I can . . . '

She went to the door and spoke to someone outside. Then she gave me a brief nod, and a kindly smile, and left. Her place was taken by Max, who crossed the room in a couple of strides and gathered me into his arms. I clung to him in a flood of tears, burying my face in his shoulder. He stroked my hair until I quietened.

'What — what happened?' I asked at last. 'Oh, Max, I thought my last moment had come. Then you jumped down. It *was* you, wasn't it?'

He nodded. 'I realised you were planning something, and I had my suspicions about Margaret. She'd been getting stranger all the time, and the business over the will only made it worse. I began to suspect, but I suppose I didn't want to believe it.'

'So I set a trap,' I murmured, 'and you watched and waited.'

'But I was nearly too late!' He shuddered, and held me closer to him. 'Mrs MacDonald and I watched her go to the barn, and I followed her. Then I realised she'd locked the studio door after her, so I tried to come in through the skylight — but it was too small.'

I nodded, remembering my own difficulty in getting through. 'So what did you do?'

'Took some of the tiles off the roof. I'm surprised you both didn't hear me.'

I suppose by then Margaret and I

had been too preoccupied! 'I'm so glad you made it in time,' I murmured.

I felt his lips, gentle against my hair. 'I didn't know you suspected Margaret, too,' he said. 'I was hoping I could stop all this some way. But after the fire, I realised it was no good. I thought you would be safe if we announced a wedding, but of course . . . ' He chuckled. ' . . . a certain stubborn little lady wouldn't agree.'

'I didn't only suspect Margaret,' I said in a small voice.

'Oh?'

'No.' I hesitated. What use to tell him that I had all but made up my mind that he was to blame for everything! 'I — er — I did think it might have been Brian. Gambling debts, you know?'

He laughed. 'Why didn't you tell me? Brian *was* in a bit of a fix at the factory, but I sorted all that out the other evening, when I had dinner with him. I lent him enough to sort things out and he's a reformed character now. He's out of the mire.'

'I'm glad of that,' I said with relief. 'I always liked Brian.' Then I remembered. 'But, oh, Max — what will happen to Margaret? Those poor children?'

'Shush.' He quietened me again. 'The boys were due to go to boarding school, so they'll be taken care of. And hopefully with treatment Margaret will be able to come home one day. She needed help, but she always refused it. Now she'll get the help she needs.'

I relaxed against him. Then, almost of their own volition, my hands crept around his neck, and his lips claimed mine.

'Can I announce the wedding now?' he demanded huskily, when we drew breath.

'Oh, Max — give me time to think! Er . . . Max?'

'Mmm?'

'We'd have to have Mother over, from Italy.'

'I'd be delighted to see her,' he said, and began kissing me all over again.

The world spun round in a warm, hazy, cozy glow. Nothing could ever spoil things again now. There was nothing for me to think about but Max — and our wedding — and . . .

I gave a squeal of horror, and pushed Max away.

'What's — what's the matter?' he demanded.

I was too busy looking for my watch. Someone had taken it from my wrist. Ah, there it was on the bedside table. I leaned past Max and picked it up.

'Penny, for goodness' sake, what's wrong.'

'Wrong!' I looked at him with indignation. 'Max Lacey, you sit there . . . on my bed, I'll have you know . . . and it's long past the time I should be up. Quick, move. Let me get out of bed. If I don't hurry I'll be late for the market.'

'The market!'

'Of course. I'm really enjoying it there. You don't think I'm going to give it up now?'

I reached up and gave him another hurried kiss. 'And,' I said as I scrambled out of bed and reached for my dressing gown, 'when you're my husband I shall expect you to make sure I get up in time. I can't be late on the job. After all, what would Great-aunt Penelope say?'

He chuckled, and ducked out of my way as I dived past him. 'She'd say. 'Well done, Penny-wise!'.'

He caught me around the waist and whirled me round. 'I always said Penelope knew what she was doing . . . and I was right. She'd be proud of you.'

I caught my breath. The last time I'd seen that indomitable little woman, she had been anything but proud. 'D'you really think so?'

'I know so. You're so like her, Penny. There's only one thing, though.'

'What's that?'

He smiled. 'You won't make me come to the market every day for three months to woo you, will you?'

I looked at him steadily, then I pursed my lips. 'I'll think about it, Max Lacey,' I called over my shoulder as I dived for the bathroom, 'I'll think about it!'

THE END

We do hope that you have enjoyed reading this large print book.

Did you know that all of our titles are available for purchase?

We publish a wide range of high quality large print books including:
Romances, Mysteries, Classics
General Fiction
Non Fiction and Westerns

Special interest titles available in large print are:
The Little Oxford Dictionary
Music Book, Song Book
Hymn Book, Service Book

Also available from us courtesy of Oxford University Press:
Young Readers' Dictionary
(large print edition)
Young Readers' Thesaurus
(large print edition)

For further information or a free brochure, please contact us at:
Ulverscroft Large Print Books Ltd.,
The Green, Bradgate Road, Anstey,
Leicester, LE7 7FU, England.
Tel: (00 44) **0116 236 4325**
Fax: (00 44) **0116 234 0205**

SUMMER IN
HANOVER SQUARE

Charlotte Grey

The impoverished Margaret Lambart is suddenly flung into all the glitter of the Season in Regency London. Suspected by her godmother's nephew, the influential Marquis St. George, of being merely a common adventuress, she has, nevertheless, a brilliant success, and attracts the attentions of the young Duke of Oxford. However, when the Marquis discovers that Margaret is far from wanting a husband he finds he has to revise his estimate of her true worth.

CONFLICT OF HEARTS

Gillian Kaye

Somerset, at the end of World War I: Daniel Holley, unhappily married to an ailing wife and father of four grown-up children, is attracted to beautiful schoolteacher Harriet Bray, but he knows his love is hopeless. Daniel's only daughter, Amy, who dreams of becoming a milliner and is caught up in her love for young bank clerk John Tottle, looks on as the drama of Daniel and Harriet's fate and happiness gradually unfolds.

THE SOLDIER'S WOMAN

Freda M. Long

When Lieutenant Alain d'Albert was deserted by his girlfriend, a replacement was at hand in the shape of Christina Calvi, whose yearning for respectability through marriage did not quite coincide with her profession as a soldier's woman. Christina's obsessive love for Alain was not returned. The handsome hussar married an heiress and banished the soldier's woman from his life. But Christina was unswerving in the pursuit of her dream and Alain found his resistance weakening . . .

THE TENDER DECEPTION

Laura Rose

When Sophia Barton was taken from Curton Workhouse to be a scullery-maid at Perriman Court, her future looked bleak. Was it really an act of Providence that persuaded Lady Perriman to adopt her as her ward? Sophia was brought up together with the Perriman children, and before sailing with his regiment for India, George, the heir to the title, declared his love. But tragedy hit the family and Sophia found herself caught up in a web of mystery and intrigue.

CONVALESCENT HEART

Lynne Collins

They called Romily the Snow
Queen, but once
fire and passion, k
by a man's kiss a
last a lifetime. Sh
would, for her. It
few months for t
stormed into her
how could she tru
So was it likely t
Conway could pie
that the lovely
wrapped about he